Shelf Life

A Village Library Mystery

Elizabeth Spann Craig

Published by Elizabeth Spann Craig, 2025.

This is a work of fiction. Similarities to real people, places, or events are entirely coincidental.

SHELF LIFE

First edition. February 11, 2025.

Written by Elizabeth Spann Craig.

Chapter One

"You've inspired us," said Luna. "That's true, isn't it, Jeremy? Ann, you and Grayson are both an inspiration."

Luna's boyfriend, Jeremy, nodded, grinning at us. "You two never thought you'd be role models, did you?"

"Never," Grayson and I chorused. We gave each other rueful looks at the unintentional echo.

Grayson said slowly, "So, let me get this straight. Because Ann and I took a couple of fateful trips to Charleston, you're now inspired to travel together."

"Correct," said Luna, her eyes sparkling. "Life's too short, isn't it? That's what I keep telling Ann. Ann would be at the library all day every day if you weren't prompting her to do something fun."

"I actually think the library is fun," I protested mildly.

Luna snorted at this. "*Books* may be fun. I'm not sure the *library* is fun when you're working there. At least, not as much for me as for you. Anyway, the point is that it's time for Jeremy and me to broaden our horizons. Jeremy hasn't taken a vacation for years and years."

Jeremy quirked an eyebrow at Luna. It was an expression Luna was likely quite accustomed to. Library patrons were always doing it at her because of her wildly creative outfits. At least, Luna found them wildly creative. The patrons might have found them a bedazzling cacophony of colors and patterns. But Jeremy's eyebrow quirk was for a different reason.

"I have actually taken a vacation," he protested. "Grayson and I went with one of our college buddies on a camping trip."

Luna wrinkled her nose. "That's not what I mean by vacation."

"It was a break from work. Isn't that the definition of vacation?"

I looked up the word on my phone. "*Oxford Languages* says a vacation is an extended period of leisure and recreation, especially one spent away from home or in traveling."

"I rest my case," said Jeremy.

Luna smirked at him. "Your case has a lot of holes in it. We're not talking about an 'extended period of leisure.'"

"Extended is relative," said Jeremy with a shrug.

Luna said, "At any rate, we're hoping for an adventure. Like what you two experienced."

Grayson and I glanced at each other. I said, "Our adventures were closely tied to murder, as you might recall."

"Well, aside from the murders. You got to explore Charleston's art district, learn about sea turtles, and do all sorts of stuff. Jeremy and I need a break from the humdrum." Luna added in a quiet voice, "And since my mom and Wilson are still so involved with each other, it's a time when I feel like I can leave her to go out of town."

We all glanced over at my library director's glass office where he and Luna's mother, Mona, were sitting. They appeared to be enjoying a cup of coffee and laughing together.

I said fervently, "I appreciate your mom's ability to get Wilson to loosen up. Whenever Wilson gets too uptight, that's when I'm suddenly saddled with all sorts of projects."

Jeremy asked with interest, "What happened with the local historical project?"

"It's on the back burner," I said. "Which is a huge relief. I've already got a lot on my plate right now."

Grayson said, "Going back to your big adventure. Where are the two of you looking to go?"

Luna and Jeremy grinned at each other. "That's the part we haven't quite figured out yet," said Luna. "But guess what? I work in a library. There are gobs of resources to help us plan a trip. I'm sure we'll come up with something fantastic."

"And affordable," Jeremy added hastily.

"The budget is always a factor," agreed Luna.

Fitz, the library cat, suddenly realized Luna and Jeremy were there. He bounded lightly over, rubbing his head gently on their arms.

"This is the sweetest cat I've ever seen," said Jeremy. "I'm usually a dog person, but Fitz could convert me."

Fitz closed his eyes as if acknowledging this fact. He had a gift for winning over even the most determined dog people, but more importantly, he seemed to have a sixth sense about which patrons needed him most.

As if to prove my point, he suddenly lifted his head and padded over to the reference section, where an elderly woman was hunched over a computer, her shoulders tight with tension. Mrs. Warwick was a regular who'd been coming in daily since her husband passed away, mostly to research medical conditions. Today she was tapping frantically at keys while muttering under her breath.

Fitz jumped lightly onto the empty chair next to her, and I watched as Mrs. Warwick's shoulders gradually relaxed. She reached out absently to scratch behind his ears while still scrolling through medical websites.

"That's a good boy," she murmured to him. "Jim would have loved you." Her voice caught a little on her late husband's name.

Fitz responded with his special chirping sound that seemed reserved for patrons who needed comfort. He settled into the chair, purring loudly enough that we could hear it from where we stood.

A gangly teen who'd been lurking in the stacks wandered over, drawn by Fitz's presence. The boy had been coming in after school recently, though he never checked anything out. Just sat in corners with his hood up, looking lost.

"That's some cat," the boy said quietly to Mrs. Warwick. "What kind is he?"

Mrs. Warwick brightened at the chance to talk about something other than medical symptoms. "This is Fitz. He's the library cat." She gave him a conspiratorial smile. "He always knows when someone needs a friend."

I nudged Luna gently. "See what I mean about the library being fun?" I whispered. "Fitz doesn't just make it less quiet; he makes it less lonely."

We watched as the teen reached out tentatively to stroke Fitz's orange fur, his hood falling back to reveal a slight smile.

Fitz was a rescue in every way, but like a lot of rescues, he rescued me just as much as I'd rescued him. Wilson had been horrified at first, since the library director wasn't exactly a cat person. But somehow Fitz had won him over, probably by keeping perfectly still and quiet during Wilson's endless staff meetings.

Luna clapped her hands together. "Well, since we're all here together, let's make plans. Not for the vacation, obviously, but to do something. What are y'all doing after work tonight?"

Luna and Jeremy looked expectantly at us.

"Actually, Grayson and I are going out tonight to see a band," I answered.

Luna's eyes widened. "Seriously? I'd love to hear a band. It's not outside, is it? I mean, it's February, so being outdoors isn't exactly my jam this time of year. Unless it's a really awesome band."

I said, "No, it's indoors. It's in that new music venue by the lake. Have you heard about it?"

Jeremy said, "Wait. Is that the building that has murals all over the outside?"

"The very one," I said.

Luna said, "Wow, I thought that was a gallery or something. What band is it, Grayson? You're always the one who comes up with the cool music to listen to."

Grayson gave Luna a smile, but I thought he looked a little tense. She realized he probably needed to finish his lunch break and get back to the newspaper office. "Thanks, Luna. It's the Palmetto Pluckers."

Now Luna was frowning. "Is that some sort of country band?"

"I wouldn't call them country, no. They sort of defy classification. They're based in Charleston, and mix bluegrass, jazz, and folk with unconventional instruments."

"Is it *fun*?" asked Luna, her brow furrowing even more.

Grayson said, "Well, it's enjoyable. But if you've had a long day at work, maybe you'd be in the mood for a quieter evening."

I looked at Grayson with surprise. Grayson was the one who always thought going out on the town was the perfect antidote to a bad day at work. And he hadn't done a great job categorizing the band.

I said, "I'd definitely call them fun, actually. Grayson and I have seen them a couple of times now. He'll be writing them up for the paper. Their sound is kind of whimsical and upbeat."

Jeremy grinned at Luna. "I'd say whimsical and upbeat is right up your alley."

"True!" cackled Luna, looking down at her outfit. "And what I'm wearing today would be perfect. Do you think they're sold out?"

"I'm sure they're not. It's a weeknight, after all, and the band isn't a huge name or anything," I said. "Is it at seven or eight, Grayson?"

"We'll probably get there at seven-thirty, but it starts at eight," said Grayson.

"It's a plan," said Luna. "As long as you're cool with it, Jeremy."

"I'm totally onboard." Jeremy looked at his watch. "Yikes. I'd better get back to the office. Great having lunch with y'all. Luna, I'll buy those tickets online."

Jeremy hurried off, and Luna, seeing some parents with small children meandering into the children's area, rushed off to see if they needed any help.

I gave Grayson a rueful smile. "Sorry if they're sabotaging a quiet evening for us. Were you wanting it to be just us? I know Luna can be . . . a lot."

"Oh, Luna's never a problem. I'm glad she and Jeremy are having so much fun together. I guess it's just been a long day."

I tilted my head to one side. "Stuff going on at the newspaper?"

Grayson said, "Nothing too onerous. Just some staff issues. Maybe I woke up on the wrong side of the bed this morning. Don't worry. I'll rally before tonight."

And Grayson did rally. By the time we arrived at the venue, his earlier tension had melted away, replaced by his usual enthusiasm for live music. The Palmetto Pluckers didn't disappoint, filling the air with their eclectic blend of bluegrass, jazz, and folk. The audience, including Luna and Jeremy, found themselves tapping their feet and swaying to the infectious rhythms.

I couldn't help but smile as I watched Grayson light up during an impressive banjo solo. He leaned in close, pointing out the intricate finger-work to me, his earlier stress seemingly forgotten. The band's whimsical lyrics and unconventional instruments—including what looked like a modified washtub bass—kept everyone entertained.

As the night wore on, Luna's enthusiasm for the Palmetto Pluckers kicked into high gear. She was vibrating with energy, her entire body moving to the music. Her purple-streaked hair whipped around as she danced with wild abandon, totally lost in the moment. Jeremy watched her with a mixture of amusement and adoration on his boyish face.

During a particularly lively number, the lead singer called for volunteers to join them on stage. Before anyone could react enough to even raise a hand, Luna had already bounded up the steps, her eyes sparkling with excitement. The band, clearly amused by her energy, handed her a tambourine. Luna needed no encouragement, throwing herself into the performance with gusto. Her infectious joy spread through the crowd, and soon the entire crowd was on its feet, clapping along.

As Luna took a theatrical bow at the end of the song, I laughed. Moments like these reminded me why I loved my free-spirited friend. Even Grayson, tense earlier in the day, was now grinning from ear to ear, worries apparently forgotten in the face of Luna's impromptu performance.

As we left the venue, ears still ringing from the music, I felt a surge of contentment. It had been a perfect evening with friends. As an introvert, I ordinarily wanted to retreat at the end of the day with a book, a cup of herbal tea, and the cat. And with Grayson, of course. Grayson was a lot more outgoing than I was, and he was definitely changing the way I lived my life. I had to admit, it was often for the better.

The next day, however, I woke with a niggling sense of unease. As I went about my usual library duties, I couldn't shake the feeling that something was off. It wasn't until late afternoon that I realized what was bothering me. Dawson Blake hadn't been in at the library the day before and wasn't there again today. His absence from his usual spot in the periodicals section was conspicuous, breaking a routine he'd faithfully maintained for years.

Wilson, the library director, walked up to me with a frown. "Everything okay? You look worried."

I said, "Well, not really *worried* yet, but a little confused. You know Dawson Blake, right?"

"Of course. He was a top reporter at the newspaper for decades. I've spent quite a bit of time talking with him. And he's a regular here." Wilson adjusted his tie, a bit distractedly. It was quite possible that his mind was possibly already on other library matters or projects.

"He's a regular except for yesterday and today. It's just so out of character for him."

Wilson raised an eyebrow. "You're thinking about having Burton run by to check on him?"

Burton Edison was the chief of police in the small town of Whitby and a friend of mine. I said, "Do you think it's overkill? I'd go by myself if I knew where he lived. Or if I knew Dawson's phone number. I don't want to embarrass him by having the police run by if everything is fine."

Wilson considered this, looking seriously at me over his rimless glasses. "I can't think where the harm is. Burton doesn't even have to say who asked for the welfare check. He could just say that there were some concerns that Dawson hadn't been following his usual schedule. And he's not a young man, of course. Perhaps having someone check on him would be a good thing."

With that pronouncement, Wilson wandered away toward his office, his library projects calling him back from whence he came.

Chapter Two

Since there was a lull at the library, I gave Burton a call.

"Hey there," said Burton. "Everything okay?"

His greeting made me think I should try harder to include Burton and his girlfriend, Belle, in more activities. Grayson and I should probably have thought to call him yesterday to see if he wanted to join up with us to see the band. Even though Burton and Luna used to date, they had both moved on and there was no awkwardness between them. I didn't want to just call Burton when there was a problem. Like now.

"I'm not sure if everything is okay or not, actually," I said. "There's a patron of ours that's a real regular."

"Linus?"

Linus Truman was most decidedly a library regular. He always started his day with the local newspaper before moving on to *The New York Times*. Although both Linus and Dawson were at the library each day at roughly the same time, it seemed unlikely Linus would have spoken with Dawson, as both men seemed to like keeping to themselves.

"Not Linus. Dawson Blake."

Burton's voice now had a note of recognition. "Dawson Blake. Retired from the newspaper. Sure, I know him. He's MIA?"

I could imagine Dawson's consternation if Burton came flying over to his house, sirens blaring and lights flashing to rescue him. Because Burton sounded like he did care what happened to him. "I'm not sure he's MIA at all. Maybe he's just caught a cold or something. So maybe keep everything on the down-low? I wouldn't want to make him embarrassed. It's just that he hasn't been at the library the last couple of days."

Burton said, "Don't worry, I'll just say I was stopping by to say hi since I hadn't seen him out and about lately." He paused. "Does Grayson know him?"

"He does. He'll walk over in the library to chat with him for a minute or two when he's here. Of course, Dawson was a reporter at the paper before Grayson's tenure there, but Dawson was legendary at the office."

Burton said, "Okay. I'll run over there real quick, then I'll call you back. Nothing much going on today in town anyway."

He signed off, and I returned to the research desk. My focus was back now that I'd handed off my concerns to Burton. I delved into research on dementia for a patron who was concerned about a spouse and looked up the best doctors in the area for diagnosing the condition.

When my phone rang, I started. "Burton?"

"Afraid Dawson's not at home," said Burton grimly. "I checked in with his neighbor, too. She said she hadn't seen him for a couple of days."

"And that's unusual, I guess?"

Burton said, "Apparently so. As you've mentioned, Dawson follows a regular routine. He's always outside on his deck in the mornings, drinking his coffee and reading the newspaper. But he hasn't been out there."

I bit my lower lip. "I see. And you couldn't see Dawson inside?"

"He wasn't inside, period. A door was unlocked around back, so I let myself in. He wasn't there. Neither was his car."

I sighed. "I think I remember he lived alone, right?"

"Exactly."

I asked, "What are the next steps, then? Is he considered officially missing?"

"I'll file a missing persons report. I'll also call around to the area hospitals to make sure Dawson hasn't been admitted for some reason. Maybe he's visiting a relative, so I'll try to find out the names of any family. Plus, I'll ask other law enforcement to be on the lookout for his vehicle."

"Thanks, Burton," I said. "I appreciate this." I wished I felt more relieved that steps were being taken to track down Dawson. But I couldn't help but feel a sinking sensation in my gut.

I heard an apologetic clearing of someone's throat. I looked up to see Linus Truman, my favorite patron in front of me.

"Sorry to disturb you, Ann," said Linus. "But is everything okay? You look worried."

"Oh, hi, Linus. I'm not sure if everything is okay or not, actually. You might help me out. You know Dawson Blake, I think?"

The old man gave me a smile. "Not well, but we're acquainted. We have the same routine, you know. And we're both in the periodical section quite a lot." He paused. "I've noticed I haven't seen Dawson in the library the last couple of days."

"That's exactly what I've been worried about. It's not like him. Then Burton did a welfare check on him, and Dawson isn't at home. His neighbor hasn't seen him doing his usual routine at home, either." It occurred to me that, when we ran our lives on the same schedule, it meant a lot of bystanders knew more about us than we might think.

Linus frowned. He said slowly, "As a matter of fact, I overheard a phone conversation Dawson was making, over the weekend when we were here." He flushed. "I wasn't trying to listen in, but it was quite impossible not to."

"I'm sure it was," I said. Linus, of all people, would definitely want to observe the proprieties.

Linus's face wrinkled in thought. "Just trying to remember the salient details. It wasn't like Dawson to take phone calls in the library, you know. He was always very cognizant of everyone who was trying to read around him. So it was something of an extraordinary moment. Plus, he seemed a bit agitated."

"Was he?"

Linus nodded. "He was asking for directions somewhere. A warehouse."

"That seems odd," I said slowly.

"Yes, that's what I thought, too. Dawson is retired, of course, like I am. I couldn't really imagine a reason he'd be asking for directions to a warehouse. It made me wonder if he might be working on an article for the paper. Maybe something freelance."

"I wonder what warehouse Dawson was talking about. I don't know of any warehouses in Whitby." The town thrived on its tourism, with its generous lake, mountains, and cute downtown.

Linus looked apologetic again. "I did overhear some of that, too, because Dawson was repeating the directions to make sure he got them correct. It sounded as if it was in a fairly rural area of town, down a narrow, forgotten road."

I shook my head. "I just don't understand that. Dawson is retired. I wonder what he was doing there."

"It did seem unusual," Linus agreed. "Dawson kept asking about zoning changes and assessed value. The sorts of details a reporter might want to know if they were investigating something." He looked apologetic again. "I did overhear him repeating the directions to make sure he got them correct. Would you like me to tell you what I remember?"

I wasn't liking the sound of this at all. Had Dawson been walking into some sort of trap? A set-up? I jotted down a couple of notes as Linus told me the little he remembered.

"Thanks for this," I said. "I'm going to call Burton back and fill him in." It occurred to me that maybe I should call Grayson as well. He knew Dawson, at least a bit, and might want to be part of this, or at least looped in.

"Are you busy?" I asked, when Grayson picked up my call.

"Just writing what's basically a promo story for the state fair this fall. Which is a long way off, obviously. What's up? Everything okay?"

I said, "I'm not sure. I might be making a mountain out of a molehill. You know Dawson Blake?"

"Sure. Something wrong with Dawson?"

I said, "He hasn't been at the library for the last couple of days, and he's usually here like clockwork."

"Like Linus is."

"Right," I said. "I put a bug in Burton's ear, and he went over to do a casual welfare check on Dawson. But he wasn't home, and his neighbor said he hasn't been. Now Linus is telling me he overheard a phone call Dawson made in the library. Something about meeting someone in an old warehouse."

Grayson said slowly, "Okay. That doesn't sound right. Was he investigating a story?"

"Dawson was still doing articles for the paper?"

"No, he hasn't freelanced for the paper since he retired. At least, not since I've been the editor. Unless he was going to send something in once he'd gotten the story finalized." Now Grayson sounded just as concerned as I was. "Are you calling Burton?"

"Right now. But I thought you might want to come with me. I have some sort of vague directions to the warehouse that Linus gave me. And my shift is almost over."

Grayson said, "I'm on my way." And he hung up the phone.

I called Burton next to fill him in. "I'll pick you and Grayson up at the library," he said, before getting off the phone.

Minutes later, I showed Burton the sketchy directions I'd gotten from Linus. "Can you make any sense of these?" I asked him.

Burton's brow crinkled as he read them. Then it smoothed. "I know exactly where this place is. It's on the edge of town, out in the sticks." He started driving in that direction.

"I'm surprised you know about this warehouse," said Grayson. "You're still kind of a newbie here in Whitby, like me."

"The only reason I know about it is because we had a bunch of teens using the place to party before we put a stop to it." Burton paused. "Hey, could you give us a little background on Dawson, Grayson? Ann and I don't know the guy really well. Maybe you can give us some info."

"Sure. Dawson's a great guy. I'm not going to say he and I are the best of friends or anything, but we're acquaintances. I always like saying hi to him when he's in the library. From the old articles I've read, he was a fantastic reporter. He was one of those old-school journalists who started out with typewriters before computers were even around."

Burton said, "How did he end up in Whitby? I'd think a go-getter like him might want to go to a big city."

"From what Dawson told me, he did cut his teeth in the big cities. I heard from other old guys who'd retired from the paper that Dawson liked his drink, unfortunately. When he got fired from a big paper up north, he ended up down here. His parents were still living at the time."

I said, "That's too bad. I hope he was satisfied with his career, even if it was in a smaller town."

"I think he was," said Grayson. "He didn't seem bitter to me. And the guy was great, like I said. From what I've heard, he could smell a story a mile away. Still, his talents were probably wasted on stuff like council meeting write-ups and bake sale copy. From what I heard, though, he'd made his peace with living in Whitby. He never misses a potluck."

I considered this for a few moments. "I wonder if he ferreted out one last story. If that's why he was going to the warehouse."

"Gotta be some reason for him to come out here," said Burton with a grunt as he maneuvered the police cruiser down a forgotten road into heavy woods.

A few minutes later, we finally arrived in front of a weathered building that had clearly suffered decades of neglect. I saw the bare bones of old timber under faded and peeling paint. Vines crept up the walls, their tendrils snaking through any available crack or crevice.

"Nice place," said Grayson.

"Yeah. Guess nature is reclaiming the building for its own," said Burton.

The building was squatting amid overgrown trees and a tangle of foliage, despite it being February.

I glanced over toward the back of the building and stilled. After a moment, I said, "Isn't that Dawson's truck over there?"

"It sure is," said Burton grimly as they surveyed the old pickup. Dawson had kept the truck in good shape, despite its age. Seeing it partially obscured by the warehouse and the overgrowth made me shiver.

"That's not a good sign," said Grayson. "Even though the truck looks empty."

"Do you have a way of getting inside, or are we breaking in?" I asked.

Burton said, "I had to put a padlock on the door when the teens were here. I've got the key with me." He pulled it out of his shirt pocket, and they headed for the door.

"Does anyone else have the key?" asked Grayson.

"Sure. County council is talking about some sort of land deal, so I left a key at town hall, too."

They stepped inside the door into what was mostly darkness, the only light coming from cracks in the roof and gaps in the walls. Like many warehouses of the time, there were no windows in the building.

Burton turned on his heavy-duty flashlight and swept the beam across the area. It was a cavernous space, dust motes hanging in the air and spotlighted in the flashlight's beam. The floor was concrete and cracked and stained. In the corner stood a rusted conveyor belt. Piles of decaying crates littered the floor. There were scattered beer cans and plastic cups, a testament to the teen parties Burton had mentioned.

"Why on earth would Dawson come here?" muttered Burton. He walked further into the warehouse, then stopped again to cast his beam carefully across the space. He paused at one point, directing the light into a specific area.

"Oh no," groaned Grayson.

They could see the slumped body of a man with steel-gray hair. A coil of wire was around his neck.

Chapter Three

B urton asked them to go outside to wait for him there. They waited back near the cruiser, Grayson perched on the hood of the vehicle and I stood beside it.

"I'm sorry, Grayson," I said.

Grayson shook his head. "It's a shock. I mean, I didn't even know Dawson well. Not as well as I should have."

"Well, from what I could tell, Dawson was kind of a prickly guy. He wouldn't have been the easiest person in the world to get better acquainted with."

"True," said Grayson with a short laugh. "He wasn't one for small talk. But this is crazy, you know? What was Dawson doing out here in the middle of nowhere? Did you see that wire around his neck? Somebody killed him."

"Do you think he was investigating a story? It sounded like he was a really talented journalist. Maybe something fell into his lap, and he thought he should check it out."

Grayson shook his head. "I guess. But why wouldn't he pass it by me first? He had plenty of opportunity. I talked to the guy at least once a week when I was visiting you in the library."

I considered this. "Maybe he was worried you'd like the idea for the story, but would want to reassign it to one of the reporters on your staff. That would make sense, right? Why pay Dawson for a freelance story when you could have one of your staff members write it."

"Yeah, that could have been the reason. Although I wouldn't have done that. If Dawson had brought me a story about an investigation of some kind, I'd have paid for it. After all, he'd have put in all the work." He looked toward the warehouse again. "I can't believe this has happened to him."

I wondered if Dawson had been meeting someone or if he'd gone to the warehouse to investigate a lead related to the land deal Burton had mentioned. "I don't know very much about Dawson, other than what you'd told Burton and me today. In the library, he was always very quiet. But did he have a big social circle? Was he connected with people?"

"Dawson was mostly a solitary guy. I mean, he knew just about everybody from working in the community for so many decades. But he wasn't the kind of person to have a group he played cards with, or anything."

I said, "You mentioned he didn't pass up a potluck."

"And he didn't. But he wasn't there shaking hands and hanging out with people. He was there to eat." Grayson sighed. "Like I mentioned, he definitely liked his alcohol, too. That might also have affected his behavior. Or made him behave more erratically."

"What about former colleagues? Did he keep up with the other reporters?"

Grayson said, "Maybe. I'll ask around. Maybe someone will be aware of what he could be working on."

Burton stepped back outside, looking much wearier than he had when they'd been walking in. "Hey there. The state police are on their way with a forensics team. I'll need to hang out here until they arrive, and it might be a while. But don't worry—I've called a deputy and he's coming over to take the two of you back to town." He looked closer at Grayson. "If you could sit on this story, from a journalism perspective, until I can notify Dawson's family?"

"Of course I will. *Is* there family?"

Burton blew out a breath. "I was under the impression there might be a brother somewhere. But maybe I'm wrong. I'll let you know later today one way or the other so you'll know if you can run something in tomorrow's paper."

I said quietly, "At least we found Dawson. I hate the thought that he could have just gone missing and never been located."

"Right," said Burton grimly. "He deserves a memorial and a burial. Not to be stuck in a rundown warehouse for eternity."

We talked in a desultory fashion until the deputy arrived. He asked where to take us and we asked to go back to the library, where our cars were. After he'd dropped us off and left to rejoin Burton, I said, "Of course, you're still investigating."

Grayson nodded absently. "Sure. Burton just doesn't want me to publish until he gives me the okay. We need to find out what Dawson was working on. Because I'm sure he must have been working on something. It's too bad we couldn't find out if Dawson had any notes or his phone with him in the warehouse or in the truck."

"But if someone murdered him because of what he knew, surely they took any notes away with them."

"True," acknowledged Grayson. "Burton might come up empty when they search the area. I guess it makes the most sense to talk to other retired staff. See if Dawson was in contact and if they have any idea what he might be working on."

"I'm just hoping they have some sort of inkling," I said. "You mentioned earlier that Dawson was a lone wolf. If he was investigating a lead, he might want to keep the details to himself."

Grayson nodded. "That's right. Maybe we'll get lucky, though, and Dawson needed to talk to one of them to find out details for what he was working on."

Grayson was already pulling out his phone and combing through his contact list. "Shouldn't we get out of the parking lot?" I asked wryly. "I love the library, but if I spend too much time hanging out in the parking lot, Wilson might ask me to come back in and work."

"And considering you've already worked your shift today, that would not be good. Where should our base of operations be? My place? Yours?"

We hadn't moved in together yet. It was mostly because we'd both been so busy with work and life. But it was also because the logistics of combining households seemed overwhelming, and there was never the right time to tackle it.

"My place," I said. "But let me sneak in the library and get Fitz."

Minutes later, as we walked into my little cottage, I was hit again with that familiar sense of comfort and coziness. The living room was a bibliophile's dream, with bookshelves lining every available wall space. My overstuffed gingham chairs and sofa invited us to sink in and start plotting our next move.

Fitz padded in ahead of us, immediately claiming his favorite spot on the windowsill where he could monitor the yard. The late afternoon sun streamed through the multicolored scatter rugs, giving the entire room a warm glow.

"Make yourself at home," I told Grayson, heading to the kitchen. "I'll grab some snacks."

I came back with a tray of cheese and crackers and some sweet tea—the perfect fuel for amateur sleuthing. As we settled in, Grayson pulled out his notebook while I curled up in my favorite chair.

Fitz, perhaps sensing something unusual was going on, hopped down from his perch and sauntered over, purring as he wound between our legs.

"So where do we start?" I asked, after taking a sip of my tea. "With Dawson's retired colleagues?"

"I can't think of another place to start, unless Burton gives us information about what he's found, if anything, at the warehouse or in Dawson's truck." Grayson scrolled through his phone contacts. "Let's see. I don't think Trent would know anything."

"What's wrong with Trent?" I asked, my mouth curving a little at Grayson's dismissiveness.

"Oh, I don't know." Grayson had the grace to look slightly abashed. "Honestly, what mostly bothers me about Trent is that he's very critical of the modern newsroom. He doesn't like computers, he doesn't like the way we source information, he thinks social media is pointless, and he disapproves of making the paper available online, even with a paywall."

"Sounds like Trent isn't much fun to talk to."

"Exactly," said Grayson. "But it's not just that he drives me nuts with complaints about modern journalism. He also launches into a litany of his medical problems when he talks to people. And his medical problems are apparently legion."

"So you're thinking Trent wasn't hanging out with Dawson."

Grayson nodded. "Dawson was way too sharp to seek out Trent for any reason. Like I said, the guy was a legend as a reporter, at least locally." He continued thumbing through his contacts. "Harry Wilcox is a better bet."

"Who's Harry?"

Grayson looked thoughtful. "I'm surprised some of these old guys aren't spending time in the library with Linus and Dawson."

"They're definitely not regulars, but maybe they've popped in and out. I don't know their names, though. Although I didn't run in journalism circles until recently," I said in a teasing voice.

"True. To answer your question, Harry is kind of a good old boy. Full of energy in his early-seventies. He's been out in the community a lot, actually, especially since his wife died of cancer last year."

I asked, "Is Harry a chatty guy?"

"Oh, yeah. No question. He'd *love* talking to us. And he's more likely to have been able to get information from Dawson."

"Were they friends?" I asked.

"Well, I wouldn't necessarily call them friends, but they were always congenial. Everybody is congenial with Harry because you just can't help yourself. I'll give him a call."

Fitz jumped in my lap and regarded Grayson with interest as he punched at his contact list and connected with Harry.

Harry clearly must have Grayson in his own contact list because I could hear his jovial voice saying, "Grayson! Long time no see."

"Hi there, Harry. How's everything going?" asked Grayson.

"Oh, fine, fine. It's a gorgeous day, and you can't beat that, can you?"

I could easily tell that Grayson was absolutely right about Harry. He seemed like the kind of guy that always had a positive spin on the world. After all, it was February, somewhat overcast, and breezy. But Harry's good humor was infectious, and I felt myself smiling.

"No, you sure can't, Harry. Listen, I wanted to bend your ear about something. Do you have any time today?"

"Time?" said Harry with a snort. "Yeah, I've got nothing *but* time. That's what retirement is all about, isn't it? Why don't you come over to my office, and we can have a little chat."

"Office? You working again?"

"As if!" said Harry. "When I say 'office,' I mean the coffeehouse. It's where I camp out most days."

Which explained why Harry wasn't one of my regulars at the library.

Grayson chuckled. "Got it. I'll be over there in a few minutes with my friend Ann."

"Ann, huh?" Now Harry was chuckling. "Looking forward to meeting her."

Chapter Four

Minutes later, I pulled the car in front of Keep Grounded, the Whitby coffee shop. Mabel Cross had bought the place some time back and was slowly putting her own imprint on the building. It was a cheerful spot with brick walls, light streaming through its many windows, inviting bookshelves, and brightly painted wooden chairs and tables.

Mabel greeted us as we walked in. We got our coffees and then joined a jolly, round-faced man with twinkling blue eyes and a full head of white hair that he kept neatly combed.

Grayson extended his hand, which Harry gave a hardy shake. Then Harry bowed at me. "My lady," he said gallantly.

I laughed. "Nice to meet you, Harry. I've heard good things about you."

"Who's been lying about me?" demanded Harry before guffawing. "Come on, have a seat and enjoy your coffee. I'm very curious what this is all about."

Grayson did try a little small talk, asking Harry how he'd been, but Harry wasn't having any of it. Finally, Grayson said, "I have some bad news, I'm afraid. Dawson Blake is dead."

Harry's eyes grew wide on his round face. "No way."

"Unfortunately, it's true."

Harry shook his head sorrowfully. "I always told him he needed to lay off the drink more than he did. He could have at least switched to coffee in the mornings instead of bourbon. I never did think alcohol in the mornings was a good idea. You've got to have *some* standards, you know."

Grayson said gently, "It actually wasn't the booze that killed him. Dawson was murdered."

"No way," muttered Harry again.

Grayson and I gave him a few minutes to absorb the news. He took sips of his coffee as he did. Then he said, "Did it have something to do with what he was working on?"

Grayson leaned forward. "That's what I wanted to ask you about. I've seen Dawson around and about and always like chatting with him. But he never told me he was working on a story. As far as I knew, Dawson was genuinely retired. Like you are. Unless there's something I don't know about you."

Harry spread his hands out. "I'm an open book. Dawson, on the other hand, could be secretive. He never did want to open up to me. But, you know, I have a gift. I don't have many of them, mind you. But I do have a gift for getting people to talk to me. It was really useful when I was working. I'd have somebody starting out saying, 'No comment,' and before you knew it, I'd work my magic, and they'd start spilling everything."

"And that's what you did with Dawson?" I asked.

"Well, I don't like to brag," said Harry, trying and failing to look humble. He sighed. "Poor old Dawson. I can't believe it."

"Did he give you any details of what he might have been working on?" I asked.

Harry nodded. "Dawson said he was looking into Rachel Campbell's death. He thought there was something suspicious about it. I asked him what, but he kind of hemmed and hawed. For a minute, I thought he was worried I was going to steal his story and run with it myself. I told him my reporting days were over and good riddance to them."

"Rachel Campbell. I don't think I remember anything about her," said Grayson slowly.

I frowned. "I don't think I remember anything about her or her death, either."

Harry said, "That's because it appeared to be an accidental drowning. That's what we all thought, anyway. And it was ten years ago. You two would have practically been children."

Grayson and I chuckled at that. "Not exactly," I said. "More like early twenties. So you're saying everyone thought Rachel's death was an accident? Even the police?"

"Everyone but Dawson, apparently," said Harry. "But when I looked up the story, I couldn't imagine what made him think there was something else there. It sounded like a tragedy. But there are tragedies every day."

I was still trying to recollect who Rachel might have been. The name just wasn't familiar to me.

Harry helped me out. "Rachel worked in the town hall. She helped the county manager's office handle their accounting and other admin work."

Grayson said slowly, "It sounds like we might want to check into her life."

Harry looked pleased. "Good for you! Picking up where Dawson left off. I can tell you one thing about old Dawson, God rest his soul. He always had a good instinct for a story. Dawson wasn't the kind of guy to go off on a wild goose chase. If he thought there was something fishy about Rachel Campbell's death, there was something fishy about it."

That was all Harry knew, so he launched into a completely different subject, choosing to pick Grayson's brain about local music shows. We told him about the band we'd seen and who else was coming into town that we were going to try to catch. Soon, it was time for us to head out.

"Hey, you've got a keeper here, Grayson," said Harry. "Better behave yourself."

"I will," promised Grayson with a smile.

"Smart man."

We walked out of the coffee shop into the chilly air outside. The sun was trying valiantly to poke through the gray clouds. "That was more productive than I thought it might be," said Grayson, looking cheerful.

"Harry's a nice guy," I said.

"Yeah, I need to make sure to spend more time with him. He loves the company, and he's entertaining to hang out with. Now that I know Keep Grounded is his main haunt, I'll know where to find him."

We walked over to my car. Grayson hesitated. "Say, do you want to go for a hike or something? I know it's not the warmest day, but I thought I could use the time to clear my head a little."

This surprised me. Usually, Grayson was eager to hop on a story once he got a lead. Especially when he hoped to run an article the next day.

"Sure," I said. "We could do that."

But as soon as we got into the car, the sky opened up, even though the sun was still shining faintly. Grayson groaned. "Never mind. I don't think the universe wants us to hike today."

"Maybe another day? We probably should give Burton a call to tell him what he found out. Unless you think he's already spoken to Harry."

Grayson snorted. "If Harry had spoken to the police chief, we'd definitely have heard about it. That would have been the first thing he mentioned. No, you're right—let's make the phone call."

Burton was very interested in our information, limited though it was. "So he was on some sort of freelance project," he mused.

"Nothing that was assigned. And nothing the paper knew about," said Grayson. "But that's what it sounds like."

"Got it." Burton paused. "I'm guessing you and Ann might be nosing around a bit. Doing your own investigative piece?"

"I'll be sure to share whatever we find."

I piped up, since Grayson had us on speaker. "You didn't happen to learn anything from the scene at the warehouse?"

Burton said, "Nothing fit for print. And you saw how he died—strangulation. Poor guy. There was nothing in the truck or in the warehouse that could help us, although it sure looked like somebody searched to make sure. No notebook, no voice recorder. And there was no phone found on the victim. I'm guessing the murderer took it off him, looking to destroy evidence that might point his way."

I asked, "Did you find any forensic leads there that might help you find the killer?"

Burton sounded aggrieved. "Whoever killed Dawson came prepared. He must have been wearing gloves. I guess the killer caught Dawson off-guard because there was no sign that he put up any kind of a fight. No blood was shed. But we did find a couple of hairs that don't seem to belong to Dawson. Whenever we do track down the perp, those might help convict him."

"That's good," said Grayson. "Were you able to speak with Dawson's family?"

"There was just the one brother, and I told him personally. You're welcome to run your story in the paper tomorrow." Burton sighed. "The worst part of the job is informing family, especially by phone. But the brother lives in Seattle, so it had to be a phone call."

"I bet that's tough," I said. The idea of being on the receiving end of that kind of phone call made me wince.

Grayson wrapped up the conversation and hung up. "Want to come back to my house?" I asked. It was still pouring down rain, so any sort of walk was out of the question unless we both wanted to get soaked. I wasn't in that kind of mood. I felt more like going home, having a warm bath, and then eating a bowl of hot vegetable soup.

Grayson said, "I'd better head over to the office and start working on the article for tomorrow. We're having some real staff issues at the paper right now. Could you drop me at your place so I can reconnect with my car?"

Once we got back to my house, Grayson gave me a rueful grin. "Today didn't turn out quite the way I'd planned. How about if we start out tomorrow with plans again and see if we're able to actually follow through with them? Otherwise, I'm going to suspect the universe is interfering with everything I set out to do."

"We can always try," I said with a smile. "I'm working tomorrow, but it's an early shift, so I'm open after four."

"Sounds perfect," said Grayson.

"Actually, I'm glad to hear you want to try to plan something. How about if we visit the county manager's office? We know Dawson was investigating Rachel Campbell's death and that she worked there. It sounds like a logical first step."

Grayson hesitated. "Okay. We can do that. Actually, there's a town hall meeting late tomorrow afternoon. Tessa Hayes should be there since I know the county was considering matching funds for the town project under discussion." He paused. "After that, would you like to go have dinner somewhere? My treat."

"That sounds great. Quittin' Time?"

Quittin' Time wasn't exactly fine cuisine, but its fried fish and shrimp were satisfying and it wasn't expensive. Grayson looked less interested in going back to our usual stomping ground, though.

"There's that new place downtown. Would you like to try it? I think it's called Capri."

I said, "So Italian food? That sounds like a plan."

Grayson hopped out of my car and braved the rain for a few seconds before scrambling into his car and driving off. I hurried inside as fast as I could, but I was still soaked when I got inside. Fitz, never a fan of water, gave me a pitying look since he clearly imagined I was suffering. I pulled off my shoes and headed straight for the bathtub. On the way, I grabbed my current book, *Nine Coaches Waiting*. I was on a Mary Stewart kick right now.

Fitz joined me in the bathroom, although he decided to stay a safe distance back. He enjoyed the steamy air after I'd run the tub and filled it up. I rolled a towel to put behind my head and then, on impulse, lit a candle. With a happy sigh, I slid into the water and started reading.

Chapter Five

The next morning, I quickly got ready for work. Since Grayson and I would be going for a nice dinner after the town hall meeting, I decided on a slightly nicer work outfit than my usual attire. I put on a knee-length black skirt, black tights, and a cheerful blue turtleneck. I topped it off with my great-aunt's old locket. I only hoped that wearing something nice wouldn't make me clumsy. That was usually the pattern for any dressy days—tear my tights while shelving books, spill soup or melted cheese of some kind on my top or skirt, and end up promising myself to never dress up at work again.

Naturally, the universe immediately made me rue my clothing choice. Not ten minutes into my shift, a harried mom with a squirming toddler accidentally knocked over an entire display of new arrivals. As I bent down to help her pick up the books, I heard the telltale rip of my tights giving way. Fantastic.

An hour later, Luna breezed by my desk with a steaming mug of coffee. "Ooh, looking fancy today, Ann!" she said, gesturing with her mug. In slow motion, I watched a wave of coffee slosh over the rim, heading straight for my blue turtleneck.

"No!" I yelped, jerking backward. The coffee missed my shirt but splashed onto my skirt instead. I sighed, dabbing at the stain with a handful of tissues. "This is why I can't have nice things."

Luna's efforts to clean me up only resulted in spreading the brown stain further. Luna gave me a sorrowful look before a dad from the children's section asked her for help, and she sprinted off again.

By lunchtime, I was ready to admit defeat. I'd managed to smudge ink on my cheek while labeling new books with call number stickers, and my great-aunt's locket had somehow gotten tangled in a book cart's wheel. As I untangled it, Linus appeared at my elbow.

"Everything all right, Ann?" he asked, peering at me over his glasses and looking concerned.

I gave him a rueful smile. "Remind me never to dress up for work again. The only reason I did is because I'm heading to the town hall meeting and then dinner with Grayson right after."

He chuckled sympathetically. "At least you're prepared for anything now. Although," he added with a twinkle in his eye, "you might want to check your reflection before that town hall meeting later."

I grimaced. "Missed some of the smeared ink, I'm guessing."

"Just a little."

After all the incidents, I ran home at lunch to change clothes completely. My morning mishaps made me look like I'd lost a wrestling match at the library, which was not exactly professional. I gobbled down a pimento cheese sandwich and some nuts, then scrounged up another outfit. I opted for a knee-length blue dress with a modest neckline and three-quarter sleeves. I scrubbed the black ink off my face, then threw my coat on to head back out to work.

The rest of the afternoon was thankfully much better. I was able to complete research for a local entrepreneur who wanted help researching market trends and potential competitors for a new business venture. A few people walked up to ask me for help with their e-readers and phones, but it was all very routine stuff.

A short while later, it was time to meet Grayson at the town hall. As I was getting ready to head out, I caught sight of Zelda cornering poor Linus near the periodicals section. Her henna-colored hair was practically bristling with indignation. Oh boy, I thought. Here we go again.

"You know how much fun you had at trivia night," Zelda was saying, her voice carrying across the library despite her attempts at whispering. "You gotta be more involved in stuff. Sitting around and reading all day isn't good for you."

Linus gave me a pleading look, silently asking me to intervene. As my favorite patron, he had good reason to suspect that I'd step in and stop Zelda from being Zelda.

I sighed and made my way over. "How about if you read a book he suggests every time he joins any sort of activity? Like stamp club or something." I offered, trying to broker peace. "You've done that before and it worked well. At least, I thought it did."

Zelda's eyes narrowed. "That doesn't sound like a good deal to me. Linus is going to choose a World War II history or something like that. It would take me years to finish it because I'd fall asleep as soon as I started reading."

Linus blinked owlishly behind his glasses. "There's a stamp club?"

I couldn't help but smile. "There's some interest in forming a philatelist club at the library. All the details haven't been hammered out yet."

Zelda threw up her hands. "See? He's impossible."

"Look," I said, glancing at my watch, "why don't you two work on a crossword together? That way, Linus is socializing, and Zelda, you're exercising your brain without having to read a whole book."

They both considered this for a moment, then nodded reluctantly. As I watched them shuffle off to find a newspaper, I couldn't help but shake my head.

With that crisis averted, I grabbed my coat and headed out. Grayson and I had a county manager to interview, and something told me it was going to be a lot more complicated than settling a squabble between Zelda and Linus.

The town hall, like the library, was on the square, so I just walked over, leaving my car in the library parking lot. The building was in the middle of the square, looking a bit like it popped out of a Norman Rockwell painting. The building's red brick had faded to a cozier color and ivy crept up one side. A clock tower rose from the center of the roof, its face visible from all corners of the square.

Inside the building was a bit of a maze with narrow hallways, creaky floors, and offices that smelled vaguely of old paper and coffee. I headed over to the assembly room, which has hosted everything from heated council debates to Mrs. Johnson's infamous quilting bee, which shall not be mentioned.

I walked in to see a fair number of people already seated in old wooden chairs facing a slightly raised dais and a lectern that had seen better days. Grayson was chatting with a member of the council. He was wearing a look I've teasingly called "journalist chic"—dark jeans, a crisp blue button-down shirt, and a leather jacket. His hair looked a bit tousled, as if he'd been running his hand absentmindedly through it.

When he spotted me, his face lit up with that grin that never fails to make my heart do a little flip. He seemed to wrap up his conversation quickly with the council member and made his way over to me.

"Ready to grill a politician or two?" he asked me, giving me a quick peck on the cheek.

"Of course." I scanned the room for our target. "Is Tessa Hayes here yet?"

"Tessa's here. She just popped out of the assembly room for a minute. How has your day gone so far?"

"Don't ask," I said with a grin. "Let's just say this town hall meeting will be the highlight of my day."

Grayson gave a low whistle. "That bad, huh?"

"Bad enough that I had to use up my lunch break to go back home and change."

Grayson said, "Sorry about that. With any luck, though, the highlight of your day will be our lovely supper at Capri."

"I'm looking forward to it. I haven't eaten Italian food in forever. I can already taste the lasagna."

Grayson grinned at me. "You've already decided what you want to eat?"

"Absolutely. That way, I can look forward to it all day instead of just the few minutes between the time I've ordered it and when it arrives at the table. I was especially thinking about it when I was eating my measly pimento cheese sandwich and nuts for lunch today."

Grayson's gaze slid across the room, and I followed it to the county manager. She was in her mid-fifties with shoulder-length blonde hair. As usual, she wore a smart-casual ensemble of a crisp blouse with a blazer and black slacks. She saw Grayson and me and strode over.

"Hi Grayson. Is there an emerging local story I'm unaware of?" Tessa gave him a grin. "And . . . Ann, isn't it? You've set up some events for me in the community room of the library."

I was impressed that she could remember my name. I'd been a bit player, and it had been a while back. "That's right."

Grayson said, "Oh, you know. The paper just likes to stay abreast of local events. You never know what will come up during a town hall meeting."

Tessa quirked an eyebrow. "True. Although I'd have thought that you'd have some sort of underling to attend the meetings for you. Kudos for keeping your hand in it."

The meeting looked like it was about to come to order. Tessa was about to move away when Grayson quickly said, "After the meeting, could we talk for a few minutes? I did have some questions I wanted to ask you."

Now Tessa's eyes were curious. "Sure. I've got a little time." She strode off toward the front of the room.

"Before we begin our discussion," said the town council chair into the microphone, "I'd like to acknowledge County Manager Tessa Hayes, who's joining us this afternoon. As many of you know, we've applied for matching funds from the county for this project."

Tessa nodded from her seat in the second row, her blonde hair gleaming under the fluorescent lights. She had her tablet out, ready to take notes. She somehow looked more like a CEO than a government official.

A woman behind Ann whispered, "Trust Tessa Hayes to show up when there's money involved."

Another voice murmured back, "Well, the county's got deeper pockets than we do. If we want to get this done, she needs to be onboard."

The chair continued, "The county commissioners will be voting next month on several municipal funding requests. Ms. Hayes is here to evaluate our proposal and answer any questions about the county's matching grant program."

Tessa's presence added an extra layer of tension to the room. People seemed to sit up straighter and speak more formally into the microphone.

When it was time for public comment, several speakers directed their remarks toward Tessa rather than the town council. She maintained a neutral expression, fingers moving steadily across her tablet's screen as she documented each point.

"The county has successfully partnered with several municipalities on similar initiatives," Tessa said when called upon, her voice measured and professional. "We're particularly interested in projects that demonstrate regional benefits."

After a while, the meeting seemed to go too far into the weeds to maintain my interest. I spent the remainder of the time thinking about what errands I needed to run on my next day off. Finally, the meeting was called to a close, and Tessa came back over to join them.

Tessa said with an expansive grin, "So, you need a quote for the paper?"

"That would be great. Let me give you some background on what I'm working on."

She quirked a carefully groomed brow. "It's not a story on municipal funding?"

"Actually, it's an article on the mysterious death of someone who worked in your office some time ago. Rachel Campbell."

Tessa froze before quickly regaining her composure. "That wasn't a mysterious death at all. It was a tragic accident."

"We believe it was mishandled as an accident."

Tessa said smoothly, "Then it sounds like a problem for Burton to address."

"Of course, this incident happened before Burton took the job as police chief. Recent events mean Rachel's death will be given another look."

Tessa frowned. "What recent events?"

Grayson gestured to me. "Ann can give a little background."

So I told Tessa about Dawson Blake, how he'd abruptly stopped his usual routine, and how we'd found him with Burton at a remote location. I didn't mention the warehouse, in case it became important later.

Tessa pursed her lips. "I see." She paused. "So now Burton suspects Rachel's death was murder since Dawson was murdered while investigating it."

I nodded. "Do you remember much about the day Rachel died?"

"Absolutely. I remember that day vividly," Tessa began, her voice steady. "It was the day of our quarterly presentation to the county commissioners. We were reviewing grant allocations and municipal funding requests. I was in the County Administration Building from morning till late evening, surrounded by staff and officials the entire time. It was impossible for me to be anywhere near the lake."

It seemed like Tessa was eager to squash any ideas that she might have been somehow involved in Rachel's suddenly mysterious death.

"That day was significant for another reason," Tessa continued. "The Commissioners were voting on our new municipal partnership program. Rachel had spent weeks preparing the presentation materials and financial projections. She was supposed to walk them through the numbers. Then, of course, she didn't show. I was actually the one who alerted the police at the time. It was so very unlike Rachel."

"What *was* Rachel like?" I asked.

Tessa smiled fondly in memory. "She was a very diligent worker, always the first to arrive and the last to leave. She managed all our grant documentation and municipal funding requests. She had an exceptional eye for detail—every application, every budget projection had to be perfect. I spoke at her funeral and mentioned in my eulogy that I truly admired her keen eye for detail. Absolutely nothing slipped by her. It's unbelievably tragic what happened to her. I was as shocked as anyone when we found out about the accident."

Grayson said in a friendly but apologetic tone, "I understand Rachel had some concerns about some financial irregularities of some kind."

Tessa froze again for just a split second. "I forgot I was speaking with a reporter," she said ruefully. "Apparently, you've been doing some digging. Yes, I heard some whispers that Rachel had concerns about some of our grant applications. But she never brought anything concrete to me. If she had, I'd have taken immediate action. The commissioners and I have always insisted on complete transparency in how we allocate county resources."

Grayson tilted his head to one side. "Is it conceivable that Rachel *was* uncovering something? And then was stopped by someone in local government before she could find out more? Or to disclose the information she'd learned?"

Tessa pursed her lips. "I'd hate to think that was the case. I have the utmost faith in my colleagues. But, of course, if Rachel was murdered, we need to get to the bottom of what happened. If there's anything in the county files that could help you, I'll make sure you have access. If you need to know about anyone Rachel worked with on the municipal funding program, I can provide you with that information."

She was saying all the right things. But then, Tessa had been in government for a long time.

I said, "Do you have any idea who might have done something like this?"

A shrewd look crossed Tessa's features as she considered my question. "I don't like to gossip, as a rule. Nothing good ever comes from it. But in the interest of information that might help with an investigation, I'd recommend you speak with Calvin Mercer."

"Mercer," said Grayson thoughtfully. "He's the guy who does all the wood crafting."

"Correct. And that's all the information I'll provide. Feel free to do some digging."

Someone called Tessa's name from across the room. "I'm sorry, that's all I have time for today, I'm afraid. Get in touch with my office, and I'll ensure the files are ready for your review. Or for law enforcement's review. We certainly will do everything within our power to make sure we're being completely transparent."

Chapter Six

Tessa strode away, and Grayson gave me a wry look. "Well, we got as far as we could."

"It sounded like you did a little research today. Financial irregularities?"

Grayson said, "Oh, I just called a friend of mine who works for the county manager's office. Have you heard me mention Jerry?"

"The guy who likes to run his mouth?"

"The very one," said Grayson with a grin. "It means I always have to make sure to schedule time out of my day to talk to him. But he does give me good information. And Jerry knows everything that happens over there. Surprising, since everybody has got to know that he's a major gossip."

Grayson's phone rang, and he grimaced. "Sorry. Let me find out what this is."

He looked at his phone screen and quickly answered. "Sam. What's up?" He paused, listening for a minute. It was still loud in the town hall, with everyone chatting or trying to influence the town leaders. The noise was giving me a headache, and I was looking forward to being out of the building. Grayson put his hand over one ear to drown the noise out. "How many work-ers?" He grimaced at me, listening to Sam on the other end. "Okay. Thanks for letting me know."

Grayson hung up. "Let's get out of here. I can barely hear myself think."

I was relieved, considering the fact that my head was pound-ing. "Change of plans?" I asked.

Grayson said, "Unfortunately, yes." His face was frustrated, and he shook his head. "The Whitby furniture mill is shutting down. They just laid off all their workers. That was a contact of mine who knows what's going on in the business world." He sighed. "Everyone else is on assignment for other stories, so this is one I need to cover."

"Of course you do. Go. This is important."

Grayson still seemed hesitant. "But we planned on going out for dinner. Do you want to go later? I'm just not sure how long it's going to take to write the story and get quotes, but I can text you and keep you updated."

"Honestly, I think it would be better for me just to have a quiet night back at home with Fitz. I'll run back to the library and pick him up. I was getting a headache in there—maybe the room was too stuffy or loud. Anyway, let's take a raincheck."

Grayson nodded, looking disappointed. "Okay. Let me walk you back to the library at least. It's getting dark out there."

It wasn't only dark. The temperature must have dropped nearly ten degrees, and a breeze was kicking up. Grayson put his arm around me when I shivered.

"What's our plan of attack for tomorrow?" he asked.

I considered this. "I'm guessing we should speak with Rachel's widower. After all, the spouse is usually the prime suspect. But I can't imagine he'd be excited to talk with us."

Grayson said, "I'll tell him the paper is doing a follow-up article on Rachel's death, since it's been ten years."

"Won't he think that's a little odd? After all, as far as he's concerned, her death was an accident."

Grayson said, "I have the feeling Burton has probably already spoken to him, so it might not be as much of a surprise as we might think. You're working tomorrow, right?"

"That's right."

Grayson asked, "Has Wilson put a lot on your plate?"

"My plate isn't too full right now, which is just the way I like it. Want me to do some digging on Rachel's widower?"

"That would be great. Do you know much about him?"

I shook my head. "I'm not sure I've ever met him, no. I'll see what I can find out. Oh, and we should check in with Burton, too. To give him an update."

"Right." Grayson grimaced, looking at his watch.

"Just go and write the story about the mill closure. I'll talk to Burton."

Grayson gave me a peck of a kiss, then hurried off to his car.

I walked into the library and found Fitz happily curled up in the lap of a snoozing elderly woman. He gently jumped down when he saw me holding the cat carrier and padded over, rubbing against my legs before climbing into the carrier.

Back at the house a few minutes later, I fed Fitz, then fed myself some leftovers that definitely needed to be eaten. After that, I gave Burton a call.

"Everything good?" asked Burton. There was a lot of background noise on his end.

"It's pretty good. I feel bad about Dawson, though. I'll miss seeing him over at the library. The periodical section just looks wrong without him. But the reason I called was to update you on what Grayson and I learned today. Do you have a minute?"

I could hear Burton walking away from the noisy room he was in. "Sure do. Let me just grab my notebook and pencil." After a couple of moments, he said, "Okay, shoot."

"Grayson did a little preliminary digging on Rachel. She used to work for the county manager's office, and it turns out that she'd apparently been concerned about financial inconsistencies."

Burton asked, "What kind of inconsistencies?"

"Something to do with grant applications, apparently."

"And you asked Tessa about that?" Burton sounded impressed at their pushiness.

"We did. She said she'd heard some rumblings about financial irregularities but claimed Rachel hadn't said anything to her about any issues. That if Tessa had known about them, she'd have made sure to check it out."

Burton grunted. "Just jotting this down. Learn anything else?"

"Tessa recommended that Grayson and I talk to Calvin Mercer. She didn't say why. Other than that, Tessa praised Rachel for being a dedicated employee. She claimed to have an alibi for Rachel's death."

"Doesn't mean she didn't hire somebody to do it. After all, if there was going to be a financial scandal at the county manager's office, that was going to make her life pretty uncomfortable," said Burton. He was quiet for a few more moments, apparently making more notes. "Okay. I better run, if that's all you've got. You and Grayson have done a good job. But Ann, be careful. It sure looks like somebody out there doesn't want any information uncovered about Rachel's death."

A little later, I was curled up on my sofa reading with Fitz in my lap when my phone rang. It was Grayson, sounding stressed. "Hey, Ann. Listen, I'm sorry about this, but somebody from Tessa Hayes's office just called to tell me there are files for me to pick up at the county manager's office. Which is kind of surprising since Tessa asked us to get in touch with her office to get them. I'm totally stuck here at the furniture mill. Is there any way you can grab those from the records room? Sorry to ask you to go back out again."

"No worries about that. Fitz and I were just reading. Sure, I'll go over there now." And I'd hurry, because it was getting closer to closing time for government offices. Luckily for me, it was the one night of the week where they offered later opening hours for the public.

I untangled myself from Fitz, who gave me a reproving look, then I headed over to the Whitby Town Hall again. I told the receptionist that some files had been set aside for Grayson and me. She led me over to the records room and swiped her badge to get access. Then she made a copy of my driver's license, had me sign a log, then walked in to get the files.

The records room was a small, windowless room with metal filing cabinets both lining the walls and in rows in the center of the room. There was a small desk with an ancient printer/copier combo. A center island served as an area to review files, and it was there that the receptionist got the files. They were enclosed in a file box with "Official Town Hall Property" stamped on it.

"Here you are," she said in an indifferent voice.

"Are these public records?" I asked. It seemed very easy for me to get them.

"No, they're not available on request. But you've both been green-lighted by the county manager. Just be sure to return them all."

I had the feeling that we'd gotten in our request for the files before Burton and the state police had the chance to.

I said, "One more question for you. Are these arranged in a particular way to make them easier to navigate?"

I didn't check my watch, but it must have been very close to closing time because the receptionist was clearly wanting to get away. She said in an impatient tone, "They're color-coded. The blue folders are public works, green is parks and rec, yellow is finance, red is the mayor's office, and purple is town council. Is that all for today?"

It certainly seemed like it was going to have to be. "Thank you," I said. I headed back out to the parking lot with the box. It looked like I was going to have some unexpected reading. I felt like I needed to delve into the material before the police whisked it away. But then, I was a research librarian, after all. It was all in a day's work for me. Or a night's work.

So that night, while Grayson was gathering information for his next day's headline, I was reading. And reading. Fitz was conked out in my lap as I sat at the kitchen table with the files. There were town grant applications and approvals for parks, youth programs, and infrastructure with letters from state agencies approving substantial funding amounts of a quarter-million to a half-million per project. These were accompanied by local matching funds documentation and project timelines and commitments.

Then there were implementation records with contractor bids and selection paperwork, and Whitby purchase orders and invoices. I frowned. I saw employee sign-offs on incomplete or what seemed to be substandard work. There were project photos showing minimal improvements, despite full funding.

I delved further into the financial documentation. There were notes in the margins of a couple of documents, and I wondered if they were Rachel's notes. Some documents were invoices from companies for vague "consulting" work. The notes in the margin said *shell companies?*

I flipped through more documents, looking for more marginalia. I found some with another group of invoices. *Double-billing?* the notes inquired.

At other spots in the files, Rachel had put on sticky notes, questioning various transactions. I wasn't sure why everything hadn't been digitized ten years ago, but it was definitely helpful seeing everything laid out in such an organized manner. Assuming Rachel had been the one to organize it all. I could see bank statements, check registers, invoices, and payroll records. Following Rachel's breadcrumbs through the assorted documents, it was clear that there were plenty of discrepancies. There was a youth center renovation budgeted at $300,000, but only showing $125,000 in actual work. A park improvement was dramatically scaled back while fully funded. Road repairs were completed using cheaper materials than what was approved and funded.

I glanced over at the clock and was shocked to see it was after midnight. Fitz was in a deep sleep, and I should be, too. It was definitely too late to share what I'd found with either Grayson or Burton, so instead I carefully arranged the files with sticky notes of my own on top of them and headed off to bed.

Even with Fitz snuggling up against me, I had a tough time falling asleep. I kept thinking about Dawson in that deserted warehouse and Tessa talking about how transparency was so important to her. My first instinct was that Rachel was murdered to cover up someone lining their pockets from the county's coffers. But I knew it might not be that simple. There was also the personal angle. Tessa had mentioned Calvin, although not how he connected with Rachel, and Grayson and I were going to see Rachel's widower, too. Finally, after a couple of hours with my mind spinning, I could wind down enough to get some sleep.

Chapter Seven

Fitz woke me up the next morning by politely informing me I might have overslept and therefore missed his usual breakfast time. I stretched and rolled out of the bed, padding into the kitchen to feed him and make myself some coffee.

Usually, I'd have been meeting up early with Grayson to work out at the gym. I had the feeling, though, that he'd probably crashed not too long ago after writing up the story and then publishing the paper.

So instead, I pulled out my laptop and set to work, finding out what I could about Rachel's widower, Andrew Campbell. Being a research librarian had its advantages. I started out by looking at probate court records, which are public. That way, I could see if there was anything of note regarding Rachel's estate. Which was when I saw the estate inventory listing a life insurance payout. The beneficiary of the estate was Andrew Campbell.

But then, why shouldn't there have been a life insurance policy on Rachel? She might have been the breadwinner of the family and considerate enough to make sure Andrew was taken care of if anything happened to her. Or maybe it wasn't that way at all.

I switched over from the probate records to other public records. Those records showed the Campbells were definitely enduring some financial stress. There were tax liens on property, a refinanced house, and property tax records showing late payments. Andrew had been married previously, too, and there were divorce records and child support orders evident. It created a picture of a man who had money issues.

My phone rang, and I saw Burton was on the line. I wondered if he'd learned the records were with me.

Apparently, he had because he was immediately chuckling when I picked up. "So you and Grayson are a step ahead of me, I hear?"

"Sorry about that," I said. "The files seemed like the next step. I've got them here and can turn them over to you whenever you want them."

"I'll send a deputy by to collect them now, if you don't mind. Are you going to be around for a few minutes?"

I said, "I'll be around."

"Got it. Did you find out anything interesting in the files? Or anywhere else?" He paused. "The state police seem focused on Dawson's family and his contacts in town. I'm thinking more the way you appear to be leaning—that it's a cold case connection that has gotten Dawson killed. But we've been facing budget cuts and staff shortages. Allocating resources to a cold case when there are current cases to be solved isn't easy."

I filled him in about the financial irregularities I'd noticed. Burton grunted. "That doesn't sound good. Also, it sounds like something that's going to require a lot more digging on my end later. Fraud can be tricky to deal with. So you're thinking Rachel uncovered these issues and decided to go public with them, I'm guessing. Then somebody in the county manager's office or somewhere else in town hall murdered her before she could say a word."

"Well, it definitely seems like a possibility. But there are other angles, too. I've also been taking a look at Rachel's widower, Andrew Campbell. There were plenty of online public records on him."

Burton said wryly, "That's usually not a good thing, is it? What kind of stuff did you uncover?"

"From what I could tell, he seemed to be having a lot of financial problems before Rachel's death."

Burton asked, "And Rachel's death alleviated those problems?"

"It seemed to. The estate paperwork listed a life insurance policy—a good-sized one. Of course, that could have been in place for totally innocent reasons. Maybe Rachel was earning most of the income."

"But the implications could be bad, too." Burton paused for a moment, and Ann could hear him tapping his fingers on a table on the other end of the line. "Are you planning on talking to Mr. Campbell? Like I said, with the current constraints, I can't really devote much time to a cold case, even one that may or may not be connected to Dawson's death. Not until the state police and I exhaust other reasons Dawson might have been murdered."

"Grayson and I are going to talk with him today."

Burton grunted again. "Okay. But you two have got to promise me you'll be careful. This guy might be very defensive about pointed questions. And he might have killed Rachel *and* Dawson."

"Grayson's planning on talking with him under the premise of doing a story to mark Rachel's death."

Burton gave a short laugh. "Not sure he's going to buy that. The whole point was that Rachel's death seemed pretty unremarkable. An accidental drowning. The kind of tragedy that happens pretty frequently."

"True. But we're going to talk with him in a public place." Which was something I suddenly realized was very important. "At the library."

"You just can't stay away from that place, can you?" asked Burton. I could hear his grin through the phone.

"Guilty," I said, laughing. "And I think Andrew will meet us. At the very least, he'll be curious. He has no idea that we're investigating her death at all."

Burton heaved a sigh. "Which you shouldn't be doing."

"We'll be careful. And I feel like I owe it to Dawson. I keep wondering if I'd been paying closer attention, if Dawson would still be alive."

Burton said, "Don't let your mind wander off in that direction, Ann. You'll drive yourself crazy. Besides, you *were* alert. You noticed he wasn't at the library, that he wasn't following his usual routine. You notified the authorities. You did absolutely everything right. For all you knew, Dawson might have stayed home because he had a bad cold, and it would all have been a wild goose chase."

"Thanks, Burton," I said. He made me feel marginally better, but I still didn't feel great about it. Which made me more determined to press forward. Whatever Dawson had wanted to uncover, revealing it meant his death wasn't totally in vain.

"I'll send the deputy by in ten minutes," he said, then rang off.

The deputy came, as promised. I spent the ten minutes before his arrival taking photos of the most interesting and revealing files and taking my sticky notes off various documents.

After the deputy left, Grayson called me. He sounded tired, but wired, as if he'd had a major infusion of coffee to power him through his exhaustion. I realized I hadn't even looked online at the newspaper to see how his story turned out.

"Hey there," I said. "How are you holding up?"

"I've been better," admitted Grayson. "It took a while for me to get quotes for the furniture mill story. It was tough chasing some folks down. Then others wanted to rant, and it took a while for me to get away from them. Then I had to make major edits to the front page of today's edition. All-in-all, it was a long night. What did you make of the article?"

I winced. "I know it's great, Grayson. I'll confess I haven't taken the time to read it yet, though. I fell down a rabbit hole with the files from town hall. Then I went down another one while looking up Andrew Campbell."

Grayson suddenly sounded a lot more alert. "Really? Hold onto that thought. I'll come right over."

Five minutes later, Grayson was in my kitchen, pouring himself a cup of coffee before settling down at my kitchen table to look at my laptop and at my phone and the pictures of the files.

"I see," he said slowly. "Wow, you did a ton of work, Ann. Thanks for checking into all this."

"Like I said, once I started delving into it, I couldn't seem to stop. Well, except to sleep." I punctuated the last bit with a yawn.

"And it doesn't sound like you slept much more than I did. Are you up for our interview today with Andrew?"

I asked, "Did you have a chance to set it up with him?"

"No, but I'm calling him right now." Grayson pulled his phone out of his khaki pants.

"After talking with Burton, I'm thinking it's a good idea if we meet with Andrew at the library."

"Ah, a public place. You're not wrong, that's for sure. I didn't spend as much time looking over those documents as you did, but it's clear he had money problems."

I said, "And if we're poking the bear, it better be with witnesses around."

Grayson took a big gulp of his coffee, cleared his throat a few times, then made the phone call on speaker.

The gritty sound of Andrew's voice made it clear he'd just woken up. He sounded pretty disoriented.

"Hi there Mr. Campbell," said Grayson in a cheery voice. "I'm Grayson Phillips, editor of *The Whitby* Times. I'm calling to see if you'd be available this morning to speak with me."

"With a reporter? Why?" Andrew's voice was now shifting from bewildered to annoyed.

"I'd like to do a piece to mark the ten-year anniversary of your wife's death. And my condolences to you. I can't imagine what you must have been going through."

Now Andrew sounded back to being bewildered. "What's this about? Rachel's death was an accident. And she wasn't somebody well-known in town or anything."

"I can explain more when we meet at the library. I'll have my associate with me." Grayson winked at me. "Should we say ten o'clock?"

Andrew made grumbling sounds on the other end of the line. But perhaps it occurred to him, especially if he *was* guilty, that he might look suspicious if he declined. Or maybe it was simple curiosity. He agreed to meet us, then quickly hung up, likely to make himself some coffee and wake up.

When Grayson and I walked into the library, Luna grinned at us from the children's area before coming over to greet us.

"Well, this is unexpected. Did you both miss me so much that you couldn't stay away?"

Grayson gave her a hug. "Of course. Why else would we be here?"

Luna put her hands on her hips. "That's a great question. Because I don't for a moment think that y'all both just want to hang out here with me. And Grayson, you should be working, surely. So what's up?"

I said, "Some bad news. Dawson Blake has died. He was murdered."

Luna's face crumpled. "What? He was one of my favorite old guys in the periodical section. Right behind Linus."

"Did you know him?" I asked.

"Not as much as I'd liked to. Dawson was private, you know. But super-nice. He'd tell me jokes that would absolutely crack me up."

This was a surprise to me. But then, Luna always had the gift of making people open up around her.

Luna now looked furious, a red flush on her neck and face that matched the red tie-dye shirt she was wearing today. "Who would do something like that to Dawson? He wasn't a threat to anybody."

Grayson and I shared a look. Luna said, "What? You mean he *was* a threat?"

"He used to be a journalist at *The Whitby Times*. A really good one. We think he was working on one last story."

Luna scowled. "Dawson was working on a story for you?"

"Not for me, no. He was definitely writing it solo. Maybe he was planning on submitting it to me for publication after he was done. But he could never get to that point."

Luna nodded fiercely. "So you're going to finish his last article for him, with Ann's help. Good for you." She glanced back over to the children's section and said, "I better run. Let me know if I can do anything to help you out. I can't believe somebody killed Dawson." And she stomped away.

"That's the angriest I've ever seen Luna," said Grayson thoughtfully.

"She's very protective of the people she cares for. And she cares for just about everybody."

"True," said Grayson. He glanced around the library. "Where do you think we should meet with Andrew?"

"I was thinking one of the study rooms. They're not big, but they're private."

A man walked in who looked like an older version of a picture I'd seen online. He was in his early 40s with rugged, handsome features and an athletic build. He was well-dressed without being flashy and still wore his wedding ring. Andrew Campbell might have been ailing financially earlier, but right now he seemed to be doing just fine.

"That's Andrew," I said.

Grayson nodded and walked over to the man as I followed. I wanted Grayson to take the lead on talking with Andrew, especially at the beginning.

Grayson proffered his hand, and Andrew reluctantly shook it. "Good to meet you," said Grayson. "And this is Ann Beckett."

I offered my hand, too, and Andrew briskly shook it before letting it go. "Now, what's this all about?" he demanded. His voice was smooth and measured.

Chapter Eight

"**S**hould we speak somewhere quieter?" I offered. It was good timing since one of Luna's patrons in the children's area chose that moment to kick off a tremendous tantrum.

Andrew winced and inclined his head briefly. I led us to one of the study rooms and closed the door behind us. We took our seats, then Grayson said, "As I mentioned on the phone, the paper is interested in running a ten-year follow-up story on Rachel's tragic death."

"Right. But I don't understand why Rachel's death warrants an article," said Andrew impatiently.

"I can understand your reasoning. You believe Rachel's death a tragic drowning," said Grayson solemnly.

"That's right. Because that's what it was. Believe me, I've had a hard enough time getting over Rachel's drowning without having everything stirred up again for what sounds like no reason at all. I guess Whitby's too boring, and you're looking for something to write about."

Grayson gave him an understanding smile. He was always so great with everyone he met. He had a gift for putting people at ease and making them like him and want to help him.

"I wouldn't say that," he said mildly. "But there is something that has renewed interest in your wife's death. Did you know Dawson Blake?"

Andrew's expression became shuttered. "Who?"

I could tell Grayson thought Andrew might be covering something up, too. "Dawson Blake. He used to work at *The Whitby Times*."

"Can't say I do." Andrew watched us through half-closed eyelids.

"Unfortunately, Dawson just passed away. Even more unfortunately, he suffered a violent death. And it appears his death might somehow be tied to Rachel's."

Andrew sat back in his chair, shock on his features. "You're kidding. No, that can't be right. The cops told me Rachel's death was an accident."

Grayson's voice was sympathetic. "This has got to be very hard for you. The police clearly thought it looked like an accident when they spoke with you ten years ago. But with fresh revelations, things can change. I thought writing a story on Rachel's death might mean new information comes forward. Maybe someone saw or knew something and will come forward now if they know her death was intentional."

Andrew blew out a breath. He seemed to try to piece together his thoughts. "Yeah, maybe that's the way to go with this." He frowned. "Does that mean the police will be talking to everybody Rachel knew?"

I'd filled in Grayson earlier on what Burton had told me about the station's tight budget and inability to investigate a cold case. But we might as well increase pressure on Andrew by letting him think the cops would be questioning him. Grayson said, "I'm sure they'll be speaking with anyone who might have information. Do you remember what you were doing the day Rachel drowned?"

Andrew nodded. "Absolutely. Of course, I wouldn't ordinarily remember what I did on a random day ten years ago. But that was no random day. I keep replaying what I did that day, thinking that if I'd done something different, maybe Rachel would still be alive." He absently twisted his wedding ring on his finger. "I was fishing that day."

Grayson nodded. "You'd taken the day off from work? Or was it a weekend?"

"I didn't need to take a day off. I was between jobs at the time, which was pretty stressful for me. I went fishing to try to relax and figure out what I was going to do next. Get my head in the right place." He gave a short laugh. "When I got home, Rachel wasn't there. I thought that was strange. When it started getting late, I called the police. They found our boat, but Rachel wasn't in it. The next day, they found . . . her. Divers had to go out."

I cleared my throat. "You had two boats? You were saying you were fishing and Rachel was out in the boat."

Andrew looked surprised, as if he'd forgotten I was there. "No, I went fly fishing. Sometimes I did fish off the boat, but I didn't want the trouble that day. I wish I *had* gone on the boat." He shook his head. "There wasn't even a cell phone connection where I was. I didn't find out what had happened to Rachel until I'd finished fishing and gone back home."

"Could anyone verify where you were? Since the police will likely come around and ask," said Grayson.

Andrew shook his head. "Nope. It was a solo trip. Like I said, I needed some time to get my head together."

Grayson asked, "You enjoy fishing? Where do you go?"

I hid a smile. Grayson was warming Andrew up again. It was a good thing because I'd seen that shuttered expression returning to his face.

Andrew relaxed a bit, so Grayson's gambit apparently worked. "I was fishing in a cove on the lake. I do like fly fishing in streams and the river, but I get good luck with large trout on the lake."

"You have to use different skills, I'd imagine." Grayson leaned forward, looking interested.

"That's right. I use dropper rigs and look for cloudy water so the fish won't spook. Then I cast quickly to rising fish. And it's good to mix up the fly colors."

They chatted about this for a couple of minutes while I managed not to nod off. Finally, Grayson led Andrew gently back on topic.

"I understand that you were on the receiving end of a generous life insurance policy on Rachel," he said.

Andrew frowned, looking defensive. "That's right. Rachel was put in the role of breadwinner for a while. She was one of those totally responsible types and I guess she thought it was important to have something in place just in case something happened to her. Then something did." He rubbed his face. "I'm sure the cops are going to jump all over that."

I said, "The policy payout must have helped with your financial problem."

Andrew's eyebrows drew together. "I never said we had financial problems. I was simply between jobs."

I nodded. "I'd have thought unemployment would have created money issues, though."

Andrew waved a hand impatiently. "I mean, it wasn't great, but we weren't struggling or anything." He made a face. "Look, dragging this time back up again is tough for me. It took me a long time to get over Rachel's death. Actually, I'm not over it even now."

Grayson nodded sympathetically. "I'm sure it must have been tough, especially getting over the shock. Did you find work after Rachel passed? I'd think that would be a way to get back into a routine and find some normalcy."

Here Andrew got rather vague. "I picked up jobs here and there, but nothing really distracted me the way I needed. Why are you asking me about my business dealings? That has nothing to do with Rachel's death."

This time, I stepped in before Andrew ended up walking away from our interview altogether. "You must have loved Rachel very much."

His face softened. "I did. We were planning on renewing our vows later that year. We were still very much in love. We had our ups and downs like any couple, of course, but her death really hit me hard."

I said, "You never thought about leaving Whitby? I'm sure it must have been tough being around the constant reminders of Rachel."

"I didn't seriously consider moving. Whitby is my home." He looked tense again. "Of course, if the police are going to try to pin Rachel's death on me, that might change things. I didn't know anything about that life insurance policy. That was something Rachel put into place without me knowing. Like I said, she was a very responsible person. I was totally shocked by the amount of the payout. I couldn't believe it was that substantial."

I said, "Now that you know Rachel's death may have been suspicious, is there anyone you can think of who might have done this?"

Andrew nodded. "Rachel was always talking about this guy who had ties to Tessa, the county manager. Let me try to think what his name was." He frowned, staring into space for a few moments. "Ethan Roberts. That's it. I've never met him."

Grayson said, "Why did Rachel have reservations about him?"

"She never specifically said he was involved in any wrongdoing, but she was always uneasy whenever his name came up. Rachel said Ethan was smooth-talking and manipulative. He was the kind of guy who got whatever he wanted by whatever means necessary."

Grayson raised his eyebrows. "That sounds like he sure could have been involved in wrongdoing to me."

"Right. But Rachel never went into any detail. It was more like he was pushy, throwing his weight around. Rachel saw right through him."

I said, "Can you think of anything specific Rachel said about Ethan?"

Andrew was quiet again, trying to remember. He said slowly, "He seemed to have unusual access to Tessa's office. And he was always around when major financial decisions were being made." He frowned, thinking some more. "She also said projects he was connected to always seemed to get preferential treatment."

Grayson and I exchanged glances. I said, "Did Rachel ever talk about financial irregularities in the county manager's office?"

Andrew gave me a sharp look. "Funny you should ask that. Is there something you know about that?"

"We're just trying to investigate different angles," I said.

"Rachel didn't talk much about what was going on at work. For one thing, she said it was sensitive information, and it wouldn't be right to share it with anyone, even me. But I knew she was getting more and more worried about going to the office. She was also having bad dreams at night. Nightmares. They'd wake her up, and she wouldn't be able to get any sleep." He gave a short laugh. "And I couldn't get any sleep, either. I kept trying to get her to talk things out with me, but she wouldn't. Rachel was always a loyal employee."

Grayson asked, "So no mention from Rachel on problems at work regarding the financial records?"

Andrew looked like he was about to say no, but then he stopped. "You know, there was one time. There was something about grant money. Some kind of impropriety. When I pushed her on it, she just said she couldn't talk about it. Do you think it might have had something to do with that Ethan guy?" His brows drew down again. "And if Rachel figured it out, do you think Ethan killed her?"

Grayson said, "We have no idea. That's why we're asking questions. But we'll be sure to talk with Ethan and see what we can find out."

"Maybe *I* should go talk to him." Andrew's voice was low and dangerous.

"That doesn't sound like a good idea," I said quickly. "We're not as emotionally involved and might have a better chance at finding more out from Ethan."

Andrew seemed to accept this, albeit reluctantly. We thanked him for coming, and he muttered a thanks in return. Grayson and I watched as he left the study room, his shoulders quickly relaxing as soon as he got away from us.

"He was happy that was over," I said.

"I guess we turned his whole world upside-down. He's probably thinking his comfortable life is going to be totally disrupted," said Grayson.

I shrugged. "Or maybe he was just upset to find out his wife was murdered when he'd thought it had been a terrible accident ten years ago."

We were about to head out of the library when Linus walked up to us. He was dressed formally, as usual, in a suit and tie. He gave us a shy smile, then said, "Good to see you two. I thought you were off today, Ann."

"Oh, I am. I just had a meeting with someone here. How are you doing?"

Linus looked a little uncomfortable. He pushed up his rimless glasses that gave him an owlish appearance. "Well, I'm doing pretty well." He cleared his throat. "I've actually got a family re-union tomorrow."

Grayson said, "That sounds like fun. Is it here in town?"

It shouldn't have surprised me, but it somehow did when I heard Linus had enough family to create a reunion. He was always such a solitary soul. He'd never mentioned them, but then he was a very private person.

Linus said, "No, as a matter of fact, it's in Kentucky." He cleared his throat once more, and I frowned. He was either very uncomfortable about something, or coming down with a cold. He gave me an apologetic look. "I hate that I'm bringing this up at the last minute. I always put off things that I don't want to do."

Grayson excused himself for a moment, saying he needed to make a quick phone call.

I was still looking at Linus in some confusion. Suddenly, a light bulb went off in my head. "You need someone to watch Ivy for you, don't you?"

Ivy was Linus's large dog of indeterminate heritage. She felt a bit like a library dog, just as Fitz was a library cat. Ivy had been hanging around the library, a stray looking for food and comfort, when Linus had brought her home with him. They'd been happy companions ever since, and Ivy was devoted to Linus.

Linus looked shy again and nodded. "I wasn't sure how to ask. You're always so busy, of course, with work. But I've been stewing at night about it all. I could have boarded Ivy. But I worried she'd think I was leaving her at a kennel for good. I'd just hate that."

Zelda chose that moment to walk up to us. Her mascara-caked eyelashes were low over narrowed eyes. "What's up, Linus?"

Linus blinked, making him look even more owlish behind his glasses. "Hi Zelda. I was just asking Ann if she could watch Ivy for me while I'm out of town."

Zelda's henna-colored red hair fairly bristled with irritation. "You didn't ask me?" Her voice grated, a testament to her chain-smoking habit. Or, perhaps, her annoyance with Linus.

Grayson joined us again although, apparently sensing the tension, looked rather sorry he had.

Linus now looked even more uncomfortable than he had before. "I didn't want to bother you. You're very busy with working reception at the auto shop and volunteering here."

"I'm very aware of my schedule, thank you. You didn't have to remind me of it," said Zelda with a sniff. "I certainly have room in it to accommodate Ivy. For someone who I considered a friend."

It seemed quite telling that Zelda was putting their friendship in the past tense. The wording was something that Linus took notice of, too.

"Of course we're friends," he said hastily. "I just didn't want to overstep. Or overly tax you. And Ann already has pets."

This didn't pacify Zelda. "Ann has a cat."

"To be fair, Fitz is so laid-back and friendly, he's almost more like a dog," I offered.

Zelda's narrowed eyes were now turned in my direction.

I quickly said, "How about we do this? I'll take Ivy to my house. Zelda, you can help me out by taking Ivy out when your work and volunteer schedule allows."

Zelda still fixed me with her stare, but then slowly nodded. "Okay. And walks."

"Of course. You can walk Ivy whenever you can." The next part of this deal was an uncomfortable one, but I was brave. "I'll give you one of my extra keys to borrow."

The smug look on Zelda's face made me hope she wouldn't have the key copied and keep it for her own. The last thing I needed was to find Zelda unexpectedly sitting in my kitchen with coffee and a cigarette.

"Deal," she said.

Linus looked immensely relieved that it was all settled. Grayson, on the other hand, looked amused by the whole thing.

I was glad to escape moments later after Linus and I set up a time for Ivy to be dropped off.

"That was uncomfortable," I said as I got in the car with Grayson.

"It was hilarious, actually. It's always entertaining to see the dynamics between Linus and Zelda." He grinned at me.

"It can be interesting, all right." I paused. "What's the rest of your day look like?"

Grayson made a face. "I'm pretty slammed, to be honest. Thanks for all the work you did on the financial records and digging up information on Andrew Campbell. I'd never have been able to get to that. I've got another article on the furniture factory closure to take care of. Plus, one of my reporters called out sick, so I need to take over his assignments. What about your day?"

"It's mostly going to be random errands, bill paying, and some other home admin-type stuff. Nothing too exciting."

Grayson said, "Got it. And, remind me—you're working tomorrow?"

"Yes, but only in the afternoon for a few hours to cover for someone who needed to leave early."

"Do you want to talk with Ethan Roberts with me? That's who I stepped away to call. I made an appointment for tomorrow morning in the hopes you could make it," said Grayson.

"I'll be there. You're really having some luck scoring these interviews."

Grayson shrugged. "This one was made under the guise of potential renovation for the newspaper building. It's a historic building, which is something under Ethan's remit."

"And Ethan was available at the last minute?"

Grayson gave me a wry smile. "His receptionist told me he could spare a few minutes, although the rest of his day was booked."

"Do you think he'll kick us both out when he finds out we're looking into Rachel's death?"

"Maybe," admitted Grayson. "But it's still worth a shot."

Chapter Nine

The next morning was bright and sunny. I opened a sleepy eye to see what time it was. Fitz was already awake and watching me intently from his perch on the windowsill, his green eyes narrowed thoughtfully. I stretched and got up, knowing he was ready for his breakfast.

After feeding Fitz and making myself some coffee, I decided it might be a good day for a jog. Jogging was one of those things that I disliked *doing*, but found I liked the feeling it gave me afterward. I slipped upstairs and changed into shorts and a tee shirt. I stretched a few minutes, then set out with my house key in my pocket.

I ran on the sidewalks since what passed for rush hour in Whitby was underway. I had enough time to get home and get cleaned up before meeting Grayson over at Ethan Roberts's office. We'd decided to take separate cars since Grayson needed to work after the meeting with Ethan.

Grayson gave me a warm hug in the parking lot. "Sleep okay?"

"Pretty well. Fitz thought so, anyway. I got the feeling he wanted to be fed earlier this morning than he actually was."

Ethan Roberts's office was tucked away on the second floor of a historic building on Main Street. The wooden staircase leading upstairs creaked under our feet. We both paused on the way down the hallway outside his office door to look at various sepia-toned pictures of Whitby's past. Main Street looked pretty much the same, aside from the horse and buggies.

We stepped through his office door, and I could smell the scent of old leather and polished wood. Sunlight filtered through lace curtains, casting warm patterns on a worn Persian rug. The dark-stained oak paneling completed the look.

Ethan, hearing the door from the hallway opening, came out to greet us. He wore a crisp dress shirt, ironed to perfection, and had calculating eyes as he appeared to sum us up. He seemed mildly surprised to see me along with Grayson, but gave us both a perfunctory greeting and firm handshakes.

"My receptionist has stepped away for a few minutes. Can I get you some coffee?" he asked as he led us into another room with what appeared to be an heirloom desk consisting of a massive oak slab with rounded edges. His own coffee cup sat, still steaming, on the top.

We shook our heads. "Got it," said Ethan briskly. "Now tell me more about what brings you here today. Grayson, you mentioned the newspaper building needing some renovation work."

Grayson gave him that boyish, apologetic grin, which had worked well with Andrew Campbell. "To be honest, the building probably could use some help. But I'll admit that's not the reason we're here today." He looked over at me.

I cleared my throat. "Grayson and I are looking into Rachel Campbell's murder."

"*Who*?" Ethan's eyes narrowed.

"Rachel Campbell. She worked in an administration capacity for the county manager's office ten years ago."

Ethan leaned back in his leather desk chair, staring up at the ceiling. "I have some sort of vague recollection of her, yes. But that was no murder. It was a natural death, from what I remember. Cancer? Something like that?"

"She drowned," I said.

"Ah, that's right. The unfortunate boating accident. Terrible business." Ethan leaned back in his chair, fingers steepled.

"It was deemed a boating accident at the time, but additional evidence has been uncovered to indicate she might have been murdered."

Ethan studied me with cold eyes. "Okay. What's this new evidence?"

Grayson said, "A former employee of the paper, Dawson Blake, was found murdered. We have reason to believe he was investigating Rachel's death. Someone didn't want Dawson uncovering the truth behind her murder."

"I still don't understand what this could possibly have to do with me. You're imposing yourselves on my time catching up in the office. There must be a reason for it. And I'll stop you right there before you go any further and say I didn't know Rachel. I'm very sorry for her tragic death, no matter its cause. However, it has nothing whatsoever to do with me."

"And Dawson Blake?" I asked.

Ethan shrugged in irritation. "Same goes for Dawson Blake. I seem to remember his byline in the paper, but I have no connection to him. You're saying he was trying to find out what really happened to Rachel? It seems to me that some truths are better left buried."

Grayson said, "The problem with doing that is that justice isn't served."

"Justice is overrated," said Ethan in a clipped tone.

I said, "You did spend a good deal of time in the county manager's office, from what I gather."

"I'm minimally involved in local politics. There's too much drama in politics for me. And frankly, I barely even remember who this woman was."

I said, "But you do know who Tessa Hayes is."

"Well, naturally. I'd be an idiot if I didn't know the county manager. An idiot couldn't get where I am today." Ethan circled his hand to indicate his successful surroundings.

Grayson's voice was deceptively friendly. I could tell there was an impatient undercurrent, though. Ordinarily, Grayson was the epitome of patience. Today, though, he was squeezed for time, and Ethan Roberts wasn't making anything easy for us. "The truth is, Ethan, the county manager allowed us to view some documents. There were transactions that didn't seem to make sense."

"*You're* not making sense. What are you talking about?"

Grayson said carefully, "Let's call them financial irregularities. Some of them involved your company."

I saw little beads of sweat on Ethan's top lip. I hadn't noticed it was particularly warm in his office. "Financial irregularities?" His eyes narrowed again, taking on that familiar, calculating look. "That's a serious allegation to levy, Grayson. The kind that requires concrete evidence. Every transaction my company has been involved with is thoroughly documented and completely above-board. I've built my reputation on honesty and precise accounting."

Ethan leaned forward to push his point further. His crisp shirt made a crinkling noise, and I wondered how much starch was in it. "I've done business in this town for many years. Successfully, I might add. If you're planning on printing accusations of financial improprieties, you'd better have rock-solid proof—the kind that would hold up to my lawyer's scrutiny."

It sounded like Ethan was ready to bring our interview to a close. I quickly said, "No accusations were intended. We're just saying we believe Rachel located some information that concerned her and may have led to her murder. The police know exactly what we do, and I'm certain they'll be coming by at some point asking similar questions." If the station could find it in their budget, that was.

A look of alarm passed swiftly across Ethan's features before it was quickly extinguished. "The police?"

"That's right. They'll be wanting to ask procedural questions like where everyone was at the time of Rachel's murder. And Dawson's, as well."

Ethan gave a puff of a sigh. "You'll have to tell me when these deaths occurred, since I have no idea."

Grayson provided Ethan with the date of Rachel's death from ten years ago, which he'd written in a small notebook. Ethan pulled up his online calendar and peered at it. "Yes. I see I had a breakfast meeting with an investor that morning. Jonathan Pierce. Apparently at Quittin' Time." Ethan grimaced at having eaten a meal at the diner. "We were to discuss a new commercial development project."

"Rachel's murder was in the late-afternoon or evening," I said.

"All right then." He studied his calendar again. "It appears I took the afternoon off. Occasionally I'll do that to golf. I'm guessing that's something I'd done that day, since it seems to be a Friday afternoon."

Grayson nodded. "And for Dawson's death?" He provided that information.

Ethan quirked a brow. "At night? I was probably asleep. I turn in early because I get up early. Besides, I didn't have a motive to harm either Rebecca or Dawson."

"Rachel," I corrected. I felt a twinge of annoyance, as if he'd gotten her name wrong on purpose.

"Right, Rachel. And I have no idea what Dawson was investigating. So you've really had a wasted trip here."

I asked, "Do you have any idea who might have wanted to harm Dawson?"

Again, I thought I saw a split second of some sort of recognition. But Ethan shook his head. "I have no idea. Like I said, I didn't know the man aside from a byline in the newspaper."

"How about Rachel?" I asked.

Ethan looked as if he might issue his standard denial, but he paused for a moment. Perhaps he thought he'd do better to throw someone under the bus instead of being a suspect himself.

"You might do well to take a look at Andrew Campbell. He was Rachel's husband."

Grayson tilted his head to one side. "So you were acquainted with the couple?"

"Not a bit. But he made an appointment with me after Rachel's death. He wanted me to help him bring in more money with investments. I had the understanding that he'd made out like a bandit from a large life insurance policy."

I frowned. "You're not an investment advisor, though."

"No," said Ethan dryly. "Andrew had the wrong idea about what sort of business I'm in. My receptionist clearly didn't ask many questions when she scheduled the appointment. It stood out because I rarely, if ever, have to tell someone I can't help them at all." He paused again. "Aside from the two of you, of course."

"Actually, you've been very helpful," said Grayson in a cheery tone. "Ann and I appreciate it."

We all stood. I said, "I was curious, if you don't mind, to know exactly how you *would* define your business dealings, Ethan. I wasn't entirely sure, myself."

"I run a property development and management company. I handle commercial real estate development, manage renovation projects for historic buildings, oversee municipal construction, and deal with property acquisitions and commercial leasing."

I said, "It does sound like your business intersects a lot with county management."

Ethan's eyebrows drew together. "From time to time. Enjoy your day."

It was definitely a dismissal.

Grayson and I headed to our cars parked outside the building. "I know you don't have much time," I said, "Do you have the chance to meet up later?"

Grayson was looking down at his phone. "Actually, it looks like my next appointment is rescheduling for this afternoon. Would you like to grab a quick breakfast?"

I hadn't been hungry this morning when I woke up, but hearing the word *breakfast* made my stomach suddenly growl. Grayson chuckled. I said ruefully, "I guess I'll let my tummy make that decision for me. Quittin Time?"

"I'll meet you over there."

A few minutes later, we settled into a booth at the restaurant. Despite the worn vinyl seats and faded linoleum, the place was as spotless as always. The smell of coffee and biscuits was inviting.

"I thought our visit with Ethan was enlightening," I said.

"Enlightening and contradicting," said Grayson, as he accepted a steaming mug of coffee from the waitress. "Andrew Campbell said he didn't know Ethan, but he clearly did if he made an appointment to discuss investments. Although I don't know why he'd have wanted to do business with him since he said Rachel had such a negative impression of Ethan."

I wrapped my hands around my own mug, grateful for its warmth. It was a bit chilly in Quittin' Time, probably from the door constantly opening as people came in from the February cold. "Maybe Andrew thought he should get someone who had a tough reputation. Thinking back to Ethan, it sure sounded like he spends a good deal of time over at town hall, even though he was obviously trying to distance himself from it. He also acted pretty defensive when I asked him about his business."

"Exactly. Like someone who's used to deflecting questions."

I said, "We should probably speak with Calvin Mercer next, since Tessa had mentioned him. Do you have enough time to run there after we eat? His woodworking shop isn't far from here."

"Sure, that'll work. There's nothing else I can plan in the meantime, not last-minute."

Our breakfast arrived—eggs and grits for Grayson, whole wheat toast and fruit for me. We ate quickly, both of us thinking about our next move.

"Ready to go see Calvin?" I asked, after taking my last bite of fruit.

Grayson nodded, standing up. "Let's hope he's more forthcoming than Ethan was."

Chapter Ten

Grayson followed me as I drove over to Calvin's workshop. The old building that housed it had once been a private home built in the 1930s. Above the entrance, a hand-carved wooden sign reading "Mercer Woodworks" swung gently in the February breeze. The shop windows displaced Calvin's handiwork, which included everything from delicate jewelry boxes to sturdy rocking chairs.

We stepped inside and I inhaled the slightly spicy scent of cedar wood. The wooden floors were warped enough that you had to really watch your step while navigating the little hills and valleys.

Grayson and I found Calvin in his workshop area, bent over his lathe. He was a lean man in his mid-fifties with salt-and-pepper hair falling in unruly waves over his forehead. His faded denim overalls and chambray shirt were dusted with wood shavings. Outside his window was a view of the lake in the distance.

He looked up when we approached. Calvin gave me a nod. He'd seen me at the library before when he'd come in to read woodworking magazines or the local paper. Then I saw his brown eyes signal recognition when they landed on Grayson.

Setting aside his work, he absently wiped his hands on his overalls. "Grayson Phillips, right? From the newspaper."

"That's right. And this is Ann Beckett."

Calvin gave me that nod again. "I know you from the library."

I gestured to the windows. "Nice view." Through the large windows, natural light spilled across his current projects. Past the garden and trees, I could just make out boats bobbing at the marina in the distance.

Calvin smiled as he absently wiped wood shavings from his bench. "Thanks. Best place in town to set up shop. Of course, there used to be more boats out there. These days, the marina's half-empty most of the time, especially in February. Now, how can I help you two today?"

Grayson said, "We were hoping we could talk with you about Rachel Campbell."

Calvin's hands stilled, and something flickered in his eyes at the mention of Rachel's name. He reached over and switched off the lathe. "Rachel Campbell. That's a name I haven't heard for a while."

"We understand you knew her," Grayson said, keeping his tone gentle.

Calvin moved toward a workbench lined with partially completed projects. His fingers traced the grain of a half-finished jewelry box. "I did." He paused. "But that was a long time ago. What's bringing this up now?"

"You might have heard about Dawson Blake," I said.

"The retired reporter?" Calvin's eyes narrowed slightly. "What does he have to do with Rachel?"

"Dawson was murdered," Grayson said. "We have reason to believe he was investigating Rachel's death."

Calvin's hand stilled on the wood. "Rachel's death was an accident."

"We don't think it was," I said quietly.

Calvin turned to face us fully, his expression carefully controlled. "I was at a woodworking symposium the day Rachel died, demonstrating lathe techniques. There were plenty of witnesses."

I noticed he'd provided an alibi before we'd even suggested he might be a suspect.

"The symposium ended at six," Calvin added. "I remember because I had to pack up my equipment afterward. It was a full day with meals."

"We're not here to accuse anyone," I said. "We're trying to figure out what happened to Rachel. And now to Dawson."

Calvin sighed, rubbing his face. "Okay. I'd like to find out what happened to Rachel, too." He gave us a curious look. "What made you two decide to talk with me?"

Grayson and I shared a look. Calvin noticed and gave a short laugh. "Never mind, I got it. Probably Tessa Hayes, I'm guessing. That woman never did like me."

Of course, it *had* been Tessa. But Grayson and I still had no idea what Calvin's connection to Rachel was. Had it been romantic? Was it some sort of family connection?

I must have looked perplexed because Calvin took pity on me. "I took a fancy to Rachel," he said. "That must sound funny to you both since I was a good deal older than she was. But it sure wasn't funny to me. I loved that woman."

Grayson said slowly, "Was this before she married Andrew?"

There was another abrupt laugh from Calvin. "Nope. I was hoping to steal her away from that guy, though. More fool me."

I said softly, "I don't think it's foolish to fall in love. It's more like an irresistible impulse, isn't it?"

His expression relaxed a little, and he gave me a grateful look. "Yes, that's exactly what it is. Although my feelings didn't help me out much, did they? I couldn't help but get frustrated with her marriage to Andrew. Andrew wasn't right for her—anybody could see that. He never appreciated Rachel the way I'd have done. Andrew was always too interested in himself. I couldn't for the life of me see what she saw in him." He slumped a little, looking defeated, as if this had all happened last week instead of ten years ago.

"And Rachel stuck with Andrew," I said quietly.

"Well, not completely. She definitely wasn't leaving him, but at the same time, she was seeing someone else. Someone who *also* wasn't me," said Calvin bitterly.

Grayson and I exchanged a glance. That was news to us.

Grayson gently asked, "Who was Rachel seeing?"

"A man named Wade Hartwell. They were having an affair." Calvin sighed. "Wade was a smooth talker and seemed to have a knack for getting what he wanted."

"How did you find out about their affair?" I asked.

"It wasn't hard. I saw them walking out of Wade's house together one time. It was obvious they were a couple." Calvin reddened a little.

I wondered if Calvin had been following Rachel sometimes. If it was just a lovelorn thing or whether it qualified as stalking. Was Rachel aware of it? Upset or frightened by it?

Calvin must have guessed where my thoughts were heading. "I know it sounds like I was following her around. But the day I saw Wade and Rachel together, I was delivering an order to a customer of mine in the same neighborhood. Believe me, the last thing I wanted was to make Rachel's life more stressful than it already was."

"Stressful?" Grayson asked. "Was that because of personal issues or work problems?"

"Both," said Calvin with a shrug.

"What was going on at work?" I asked.

Calvin considered the question. "I don't really know. I just know it was stressing her out."

I asked, "How did you and Rachel meet? It doesn't seem as if your paths would ordinarily have crossed often."

"No, I suppose it wouldn't seem that way. Since I'm a traditional craftsman preserving historic techniques, I was at the town hall a good deal to apply for arts and cultural preservation grants. Rachel handled grant documentation for the county. I was there fairly often to discuss applications." He colored. "Maybe more often than was strictly necessary."

"Did you ask Rachel out?" I asked.

Calvin looked down. "We never had time for me to do that. I mean, I was seeing her at the town hall, so it wasn't the best place to ask her." He gave a short laugh. "It hurt a lot more when I realized Rachel was involved with Wade Hartwell. Maybe she was looking for something she wasn't finding with

Andrew. Wade was the kind of guy who was just using her, though. I tried warning her, but she wouldn't listen."

I said softly, "You must have been devastated when Rachel died."

"It was awful," said Calvin quietly. "I couldn't believe it at first. Nothing about it seemed right."

"Did Rachel usually go out on the boat?" Grayson asked, leaning forward slightly.

"No. Not as far as I understood, anyway. We'd engage in small talk at town hall, Rachel and I. She'd mentioned before that Andrew had a boat he'd go fishing on. She never mentioned using it, especially solo. And I know Rachel was a great swimmer. She said she was on the swim team when she was in high school, just like me. It was something we had in common."

They must not have had *too* much in common if Calvin was having to reach all the way back to high school to find similarities.

I asked, "Was there anything different about Rachel in the days leading up to her death?"

Calvin nodded wearily. "Absolutely. She was a lot quieter and a lot more stressed out. When she was stressed, she didn't talk much. I figured she was realizing she was stuck in a bad marriage. Maybe that was just wishful thinking. It was probably her work that was making her feel stressed. Rachel always had a ton in her inbox."

"Do you have any idea who might have wanted to murder Rachel?" I asked gently.

Calvin threw up his hands. "It's got to be one of the people around her, right? My guess is her husband Andrew, Wade Hartwell, or maybe Julie Hartwell."

Grayson lifted an eyebrow. "Julie Hartwell? Wade was married?"

"Absolutely. And it's not the first time Wade has strayed. Like I said, he was bad news for Rachel. But Julie always stuck with him." Calvin ducked his head, looking embarrassed. "I'm ashamed to admit I told Julie about Wade's affair with Rachel." He lifted his head again, looking defensive. "I'm not proud of what I did. I was hoping Julie would blow up at Wade and he'd drop Rachel. Instead, Julie blew up at me."

"Julie didn't believe you?" I asked.

Calvin gave me a tired look. "Oh, she believed me, all right. But she told me her marriage was none of my business. She was right about that, of course." He shrugged. "I thought Julie would be furious at Rachel. The two of them were friends. It's their friendship that likely brought Rachel into Wade's orbit to begin with."

Calvin was quiet for a few moments. After a while, I asked, "Did you know Dawson Blake very well?"

Calvin shook his head. "No, we didn't run in the same circles, so we were just acquaintances. I was sorry to read about his death, though. He took pictures sometimes for the paper for the downtown arts and crafts fairs. I just passed the time of day with him when he did." He frowned. "So you're saying Dawson's death was connected to Rachel's. That they were both murdered?"

"That's what it's looking like," said Grayson.

Calvin shook his head. "Awful." Then he glanced at his well-worn watch. "I hate to cut this short, but I've got a project to finish up so that I can stay on track to deliver it. But if I can help you put whoever killed Rachel behind bars, I'll do whatever it takes. Just let me know."

We walked ourselves out and headed for our separate cars. Grayson gave me a hug before I climbed into the driver's seat. "At some point, things will settle down on my end. Probably right when things start ramping up on yours," he said in a rueful voice.

"It's the way life is," I said with a smile and a shrug. "Good luck with everything today."

"What does the rest of your morning look like?"

I said, "Well, I *think* Linus is going to come by with Ivy so I can watch her while he's out of town. But he was so very reticent to get help that I'm not totally sure that's the case."

"Ivy might be meeting Linus's extended family at the reunion?" asked Grayson with a grin.

"It could happen."

Chapter Eleven

A few minutes later, I was back at the house. Fitz was happy to see me. He was curled up in a sunbeam, relaxed and happy. But then, Fitz was nearly always relaxed and happy.

"Are you going to be okay having a houseguest for a little while?" I asked him.

Fitz gave me a feline smile. He was always very laid back with dogs and other cats. It was part of what made him such a remarkable boy.

I was giving up on Linus when I finally heard a gentle tap at the door after a while. I opened it to find Linus standing there, a well-behaved Ivy on a leash and with that same apologetic look on his face that he'd had at the library. Of course, he was in his usual suit and sported a red tie.

"You're absolutely sure this is okay, Ann?" he asked anxiously. "Fitz won't mind?"

"Fitz will love it. Come on inside and let's see how they do together."

The nice thing was that Ivy was a very polite animal. She practically tiptoed inside my cottage, looking around her with interest. She recognized Fitz, who was still happily lounging in the sunbeam, and stopped short before watching him curiously. He lifted his head, gazed thoughtfully at Ivy, then lay his head down again.

Linus looked relieved. "Fitz doesn't seem to mind. This is his house and the last thing I want to do is stress him out in it."

"That would be impossible. Don't worry about a thing, Linus. Just drive safely and enjoy your family reunion. Do you have Ivy's food?"

Of course he did. Linus even had carefully divided it by meal, each portion in a zipper bag labeled with the day of the week and whether it was the morning or evening meal. Some bags had sprinkles on the food.

"Ivy has a probiotic once a day, so I added it in."

I said, "You've made it all very easy for me."

Linus gave me a smile. "Thank you, Ann. I wouldn't have enjoyed myself a bit if I'd known Ivy was in a kennel." He paused. "I read the story in the paper about Dawson. I was very sorry to hear the news."

I winced. I'd meant to get in front of the news and let Linus know in a gentler way. He and Dawson weren't close, but they were acquainted. "I'm so sorry I didn't let you know before you saw it in the paper. But Linus, if you hadn't told me what you'd overheard in terms of where Dawson had been heading to meet someone, it might have been a lot longer before he was found. Thanks for looking out for him."

Linus looked pleased. "I'm glad to help, even in a small way. I just wish it hadn't been too late."

We chatted for another few minutes before I gently sent him on his way. It sounded like he had a long drive ahead of him.

I'd barely gotten Ivy settled when there was another knock at the door, this one more emphatic. Zelda stood there, hands on her hips.

"I can't believe Linus asked you instead of me to watch Ivy," she announced without preamble, stepping inside. She took in the sight of Ivy and Fitz peacefully coexisting. "Although I have to admit, your house does look like some sort of pet sanctuary."

"Would you like to help walk her?" I offered, remembering our arrangement. "I've got an extra key for you."

Zelda's expression brightened slightly, but she tried to maintain her aggrieved air. "Well, I suppose someone needs to make sure she gets proper exercise. And speaking of exercise, when was the last time anyone trimmed those hedges next door? The whole neighborhood's going to pot."

Ivy padded over to investigate our visitor. Zelda's stern expression softened as she reached down to pat the dog's head. "At least Linus takes good care of you. Though I don't know why he dresses up in a suit to walk you. Completely impractical."

I handed Zelda the key, trying not to flinch as I imagined her making copies. "I've got Ivy's schedule written down, and Linus left detailed instructions about—"

"Oh please," Zelda interrupted, waving away my words with her hand. "I know how to walk a dog. Besides, this will give me a chance to keep an eye on things. Did you know Mrs. Wilkes down the street has her garbage cans out a full day early?"

"And another thing," Zelda continued, settling uninvited into one of my gingham chairs. "Those new people on Oak Street haven't pressure-washed their driveway since moving in.

Not once." She leaned forward. "Have you thought about joining the HOA board yet?"

"Still no time for that," I said quickly. "Between the library and—"

"The library! That's another thing. Wilson's got you working too hard. I was in there yesterday and that printer was acting up again. He's always got you wrangling with it instead of calling the maintenance guy. Somebody needs to tell him to replace that ancient thing."

I watched as Ivy settled onto the scatter rug near Zelda's feet. Even the dog seemed resigned to a lengthy discourse on various problems in town.

"You know what you need?" Zelda asked, though I was quite sure she was going to tell me regardless of my response. "You need to get more involved in the community. I don't mean at work, but closer to home. Like me. I see everything that goes on around here. Take this morning, for instance. You won't believe what I saw."

Just then, Ivy perked up her ears and gave a hopeful look at her leash hanging by the door.

"Oh! Would you like to take her for her walk now?" I asked, perhaps a bit too eagerly.

"Well, I suppose I should," Zelda said, standing up. "Somebody needs to keep an eye on things. Did you know the Sullivans installed a satellite dish without getting proper approval?"

After Zelda left with Ivy, I settled in to do some research on my laptop. I still had those photos I'd taken of the files from town hall before Burton's deputy collected them. If Rachel had discovered financial irregularities, I wanted to understand exactly what she might have found.

I was deep in municipal records when Zelda burst back through my front door, bringing a blast of cold air with her. Ivy looked perfectly content, but Zelda was agitated.

"You won't believe what I just saw," she announced, not bothering with a greeting. She unclipped Ivy's leash while continuing, "First, the Hendersons still have their Christmas lights up. In February! But that's not the worst part."

I saved my work and closed the laptop. "What's the worst part?"

"There's this young teenage boy skulking around. Must be playing hooky from school because he should definitely be in class. He was trying car door handles in the driveways." Zelda paused to cough. Maybe the brisk walk had been more exercise than she was used to. Or maybe her lungs were compromised by her cigarette habit. "I called Burton about it."

"What did Burton say?"

"He said he was handling a murder investigation," Zelda sniffed indignantly. "As if that's more important than someone breaking into cars in our neighborhood. But I kept my eye on this kid. He looked like he was at loose ends. The kind that could get into real trouble."

I noticed that despite her complaints, there was a note of genuine concern in Zelda's voice.

"You seem worried about him," I said carefully.

Zelda immediately started coughing again before saying, "Well, somebody should be. He's too young to be getting mixed up in crime." She hesitated. "He looked hungry, maybe. Or lost. Not like your typical delinquent."

I watched as Ivy settled onto her bed, but kept her eyes trained on Zelda. Even the dog seemed interested in the story.

"Did you talk to him?" I asked.

"I tried. Called out to him, but he took off running." Zelda's eyes narrowed. "That's suspicious behavior right there." She paused again, fiddling with her cigarette. "But the way he ran. It wasn't like he was trying to get away with something. More like he was scared."

This was a different side of Zelda. Usually, her neighborhood observations came wrapped in criticism and judgment. But there was some genuine worry in her voice now.

"You know what else?" She leaned forward in her chair. "I saw him looking in the window at Quittin' Time earlier. Just staring at people eating. Then he checked his pockets like he was counting change or something." She shook her head. "That's not right. A kid that age should be in school, getting a proper lunch."

"I could talk to Burton," I offered. "When he's not focused on Dawson's murder, I mean."

"Oh, I'll be talking to Burton again myself," said Zelda grimly. "But I suppose he does have his hands full right now."

"Has anyone else in the neighborhood noticed him?" I asked.

"They should have. But you know how people are these days. Too wrapped up in their phones to notice what's happening right in front of them. Not like me. I notice everything."

That was certainly true. Sometimes too true.

"Well, Ivy and I will do another patrol this afternoon," Zelda announced, standing up. "After my shift at the garage." She looked down at Ivy, who was still watching her alertly. "We make a good team, don't we, girl?"

I walked her to the door, grateful my uninvited guest was leaving. "Thanks for helping with Ivy, Zelda. I know Linus appreciates it."

"Hmph. He's got a funny way of showing it." But she didn't sound quite as put out as she had earlier. "I'll be by around four. And Ann?" She paused in the doorway. "Keep an eye out for that boy. Something's not right there."

After she left, I opened a few windows despite the February chill and went back to my research. But I found myself thinking about the boy Zelda had seen. She might be overly zealous about neighborhood rules, but her instincts about people were usually good. And there was something about the way she'd described him that nagged at me. Maybe I'd mention it to Burton after all.

Which reminded me I should probably check in with Burton. I gave him a call, which went to voicemail. A few minutes later, he called me back.

"Ann," he said. "How are things looking on the cold case front?"

"Just wanted to fill you in. Grayson and I spoke to Ethan Roberts and Calvin Mercer. Ethan told us Andrew Campbell came to see him after Rachel's death, wanting investment advice. But when we interviewed Andrew, he claimed he didn't know Ethan at all."

"Hmm," said Burton. "Okay. That's a pretty big contradiction."

"There's more, too. Calvin Mercer revealed Rachel was having an affair with Wade Hartwell. According to Calvin, Rachel was a strong swimmer; she'd been on the swim team in high school. It just makes her drowning seem even more suspicious."

"What was Calvin's connection to Rachel again?"

"He was in love with her. He'd met her when he was applying for arts and cultural preservation grants at town hall. Calvin made it sound like he'd created reasons to be at town hall more often than necessary, just to see her. According to Calvin, Rachel clearly wasn't interested, but that didn't stop him from carrying a torch."

"Did he seem bitter about the rejection?" asked Burton.

"More sad than bitter. But he did point us toward three people we should look into. First, there's Andrew Campbell. Calvin said he never appreciated Rachel, that he was too wrapped up in himself. Then there's Wade Hartwell, who Calvin says was having an affair with Rachel. Calvin painted him as a smooth talker who treated Rachel like just another conquest."

"And the third?" asked Burton.

"Julie Hartwell, Wade's wife. Calvin said she knew about the affair. And speaking of affairs, that's another thing that bothers me about Rachel's death. Why would she have been on Andrew's boat alone that day? Calvin said she never did that."

"Did Calvin have an alibi?" asked Burton.

"He volunteered one before we even asked. He said he was at a woodworking symposium until four that afternoon. But he was pretty quick to point out he was alone after that, with no witnesses."

"Gotcha. What did you learn from Ethan Roberts?"

I said, "Ethan tried to act like he barely remembered Rachel, but he seemed to know a lot about what happened after her death. He told us Andrew Campbell came to see him, wanting investment advice after getting Rachel's life insurance payout."

"But you said earlier that Andrew denied knowing Ethan?"

"Exactly. When we interviewed Andrew, he claimed he'd never met Ethan. But Ethan was very specific about Andrew making an appointment to see him. He said it stood out because he had to turn Andrew away; Ethan's company handles property development and municipal construction, not investments."

I heard Burton's pen scratching. "What else about Ethan?"

"He got really defensive when I asked about his business dealings with the town. He handles all these municipal projects: commercial real estate, historic building renovations, and property acquisitions. But when I pointed out how much his work intersects with county management, he got very defensive, even threatening to involve his lawyers."

"Sounds like you hit a nerve," said Burton.

"There's one more thing. When we brought up Dawson's murder, I could swear I saw something flash across his face. Recognition, maybe? But then he claimed he barely knew Dawson. That he just remembered seeing his byline in the paper from time to time."

"Let me get this straight," Burton said. "We've got Andrew Campbell lying about knowing Ethan, Ethan getting defensive about his municipal dealings, Calvin in love with Rachel but pointing fingers at three other people, and everybody claiming they barely knew Dawson despite evidence suggesting otherwise."

"That about sums it up," I said.

"And Rachel somehow stumbled onto something in the county records that got her killed. But was it the financial stuff we already know about, or something else?"

"That's what we're trying to figure out. One thing's clear though. Dawson was getting close to answers, and somebody didn't like that."

Burton was quiet for a moment. I could hear him tapping his fingers on what was probably his desk. "Are you planning on talking to Andrew Campbell again? Like I said, with the current constraints, I can't really devote much time to a cold case, even one that may or may not be connected to Dawson's death. Not until the state police and I exhaust other reasons Dawson might have been murdered."

"Grayson and I will keep digging," I assured him.

Burton grunted again. "Okay. But you two have got to promise me you'll be careful. This guy might be very defensive about pointed questions. And he might have killed Rachel *and* Dawson."

I told him we'd be careful. Then I remembered I was going to tell him about the boy Zelda had seen trying to open car doors and peering into Quittin' Time. Something made me hesitate, though. And, by the time I opened my mouth again, Burton had rung off.

Chapter Twelve

The rest of the day was spent getting Ivy acclimated, reading, and doing some chores at home. I'm not one to mind a quiet day, of course. It meant I had time to curl up with my book and love on both a dog *and* a cat. Which was pretty much heaven for me.

I also thought a bit about what I'd learned. I reflected, in particular, on Julie Hartwell, the wife of the man Rachel was having the affair with. When I pulled her up online, I recognized a picture of her on social media. She went to the gym where Grayson and I worked out, and I saw her there regularly for a class of some kind. With Grayson so swamped with work and, considering the fact I hadn't been able to make it to the gym lately, I decided to go early the next morning before work.

So the next morning, I woke up very early, took Ivy for a quick walk, fed the animals, gulped down a little whole wheat toast with a smidge of butter, then headed off in the darkness to the gym.

The trick was to loiter, waiting for Julie, without looking as if I was loitering at all. It occurred to me I'd likely be able to have a much longer chat with Julie Hartwell if I waited until after her group class was finished. So I did my regular workout, keeping an eye on the time.

Then I walked back out near the doors to the group classes. Sure enough, Julie came out. She was around forty years old with her brown hair tied up in an elegant twist. She was wearing upmarket yoga clothing. "Thanks for the workout," she said to the instructor, who was standing at the door as everyone walked out. "You've pretty much done me in for the day."

The instructor said, "Remember, yoga is a personal journey."

"Oh, I know all about personal journeys," said Julie wryly. "And setbacks."

She walked toward me, and suddenly I wasn't sure exactly how to proceed. It was easier when Grayson was with me and acting on behalf of the newspaper.

Fortunately, Julie stopped short and did the work for me. "Ann, right?" she asked. "From the library."

Considering I was a fixture there, I was never really surprised when people knew who I was. And now I remembered I knew her from the library as well as the gym. "That's right," I said. "You usually come by for one of our book clubs, don't you?"

Julie made a face. "Well, I did, but then the club I was part of wasn't picking books that really appealed to me." She gestured over to the smoothie café which operated in a small space in the gym. "I'm heading over to get an herbal tea. Want to join me? Maybe you'll have some suggestions about a club that might work better for me."

I joined her, glad that I wasn't opening the library that day, but working later in the morning. I ordered a kale smoothie and sat down with Julie, who was quaffing her herbal tea. Then I gave her the lowdown on the various book clubs and what I made of them. Some of them were library-led and others were patron-led.

"Got it," said Julie. She paused. "I don't want to be nosy, but aren't you dating the newspaper editor? Grayson, isn't it?"

I nodded. "That's right."

Julie leaned back in her seat. "That must always be interesting. There's been so much going on lately, locally." She paused. "I read about the murdered journalist in the paper. That was awful. You always think these small towns are safer than the bigger ones. Then something like that happens."

"Did you know Dawson Blake?" I asked.

"Was that his name? No, I'm afraid I didn't know him. He was an older man, wasn't he?"

I said, "He was retired." I paused. "It actually seems as if he might have been connected with Rachel Campbell. I believe you might have known her."

Julie froze. "Rachel? But how could Dawson have been connected to Rachel? She died years ago."

"A decade ago, yes. It looks as if Dawson was investigating her death. He did some investigative journalism in his time."

Julie's neat eyebrows pulled together. "I just don't understand this at all. Rachel's death was a terrible accident. And yes, I knew her. We were friends. She drowned off the side of the boat she and Andrew owned."

"Apparently, her death might not have been an accident at all. Dawson was looking to see if it might have been murder." I paused, letting her absorb that for a moment. "This is hard to ask, but were you and Rachel still friends at the end? Before her death?"

Julie pressed her lips together in dissatisfaction, whether at me or at the issue. "I suppose people in Whitby have been gossiping, as usual. That's so tiresome, but I should know how this town operates by now. No, Rachel and I weren't really friends at the end. I was disappointed that my husband was having an affair with my friend. I naively thought friends didn't behave like that. But I'd never have done anything to harm either one of them."

I took a big sip from my smoothie. "And your husband? Do you think he'd have harmed Rachel?"

"Wade?" Julie snorted. "For heaven's sake, no. He was besotted with her at the time. Besides, he was out of town on business when Rachel died, so he couldn't have been involved." She paused and then said with dignity, "And before you ask, Wade and I are still married."

"That's very generous and forgiving of you," I said.

Julie searched my face suspiciously before apparently seeing that I was being genuine. "Well, I'm not saying it was easy. I've struggled for years to come to terms with the betrayal of trust. But I certainly would never resort to violence or revenge of any kind." She frowned. "You're not saying the police are reopening the investigation into Rachel's death."

"It doesn't sound as if there was much of an investigation at all. It seemed it was immediately deemed an accident."

Julie nodded. "That's true. I just wish the police wouldn't start digging everything up again."

"If they do, can't you just tell them where you were the day Rachel died? That should stop their prying."

Julie shrugged. "Sure. I remember it pretty well because I was quite shaken up when I heard Rachel had drowned. I'd been at the library. At a book club meeting. Our group was reading *Pride and Prejudice*. It was when the club was still reading books that I enjoyed. I even remember we had a lively discussion about Mr. Darcy and the various film and television adaptations of the book."

It was far from an alibi. The book clubs only have the room for a couple of hours, tops. The meetings rarely, if ever, run that long. And where was Julie in the late-afternoon or evening, when Rachel had apparently died?

I asked her those questions, and Julie said sharply, "That afternoon, I was at home, doing things like housework and paying bills. Look, I understand why you might suspect me, given the circumstances. But I didn't have either the opportunity or the desire to harm Rachel. And I'm appalled that somebody actually did harm her."

"I know this is new information to you, but is there anyone you can think of who might have had a reason to murder Rachel?"

Julie didn't hesitate before replying. "Andrew Campbell, of course. It's always the husband, isn't it? He apparently made a good deal of money off her death. He's been something of the merry widower."

Of course, I'd seen Rachel's estate paperwork showing he'd profited off a life insurance policy on her. But I still wanted a glimpse into the before-and-after of his lifestyle change. "Did he?" I asked.

"Absolutely. I'm not saying that they were in dire straits before Rachel's death. But local gossips were saying Andrew wasn't great with money. And Rachel mentioned much the same to me, when we were still talking to each other daily."

"What would Rachel say?" I asked.

Julie shrugged. "Just that Andrew wasn't great at business. And that he wasn't great at financial matters, either. I figured he was blowing money on things. After all, he'd bought a boat, although he'd made Rachel take out the loan, since he had too much debt to qualify." She shook her head. "Poor Rachel. I know the boat factored into her death. I did think it was a little weird that she'd drown. From what I understood, she was an excellent swimmer."

Julie stood, and I did the same, hastily taking a last gulp from my kale smoothie. "Now I really need to go. It was good seeing you, Ann. Thanks for all the information on the book club. And, I suppose, on Rachel's death, too. At least it's good to know what really happened."

I needed to get going, too. I left shortly after Julie did and headed home to get ready for work and take Ivy out for a quick walk, which she eagerly acquiesced to. It was speedier than the walks Linus usually took her on—there was maybe less sniffing around, but decidedly more cardio. Not long after, I was driving to the library with Fitz in tow in his carrier.

The library was busy when I got there, and I scrambled to help with patrons who were looking for help finding books, researching and applying for jobs, and needing technology help.

The ones who needed tech help reminded me I should schedule another free tech day at the library. Our young volunteer, Timothy, was great to help with those.

Finally, there was a lull and Luna came over to the reference desk. As usual, she was colorfully attired, this time in a rainbow-striped cardigan over a polka-dot top. Somehow, it all managed to coordinate with her signature purple-streaked hair.

"Ready for your lunch break?" I asked her.

"Ready for Jeremy to show up so I can take it," said Luna in a good-humored grumble. "We're meeting up for lunch. Like a date."

"I'm here, I'm here," said Jeremy, sounding breathless and looking somewhat guilty. "Sorry, somebody was asking me a question back at the office, and it took longer than it should have." He held up takeout bags. "I didn't want to cut into your lunch hour, so I picked up our favorites at the deli." He gave Luna a suddenly contrite look. "I hope that's okay."

Luna brightened at the aroma coming from the bags. "That's not just okay, that's perfect."

"How are things going with your vacation planning?" I asked.

"Oh right, the vacation," said Jeremy, looking guilty once again.

"No progress has really been made on that," said Luna, making a face.

Jeremy said, "We really *wanted* to make progress, though."

"Yes," agreed Luna. "We were totally enthusiastic about it."

"Then we got a little overwhelmed by options," said Jeremy.

Luna added, "Which is when we started binge-watching our favorite show online."

"Which perfectly encapsulates how we got to this point," said Jeremy.

I said, "Well, like I mentioned last time, the library is full of travel guides. How about if you both make a top-ten bucket list? Then you can compare them to find overlapping destinations."

"Perfect!" said Luna, beaming at me. "That's exactly what we'll do. Just as soon as we eat this delicious-smelling lunch. I'm so hungry right now that I could chew through the plastic bag."

After Luna and Jeremy had disappeared into the breakroom to eat their lunch, I worked on social media posts for the library for a few minutes. Fitz came over, tail swishing lightly, to see what I was doing.

"Want to model today?" I asked, half-distractedly. Fitz, as the library cat, was often pictured in our social media to represent Whitby Library. And, as expected, they were the most-viewed and most-shared posts I posted.

But Fitz seemed a little distracted himself. He was looking across the library at Luna's mother, Mona. Mona was often at the library knitting, taking part in a book or film club, and reading books. But now, she was participating in none of those activities. In fact, she was stretching at a most unnatural angle, looking as if she was trying to peer at an upper shelf in the non-fiction area.

I walked over to see if I could give her a hand, Fitz padding along behind me.

"Need me to reach something for you, Mona?" I asked.

Mona put her arm back down, rubbing it a little and looking up with frustration at the top shelf. "Luna told me about Dawson yesterday. I hate to hear it. Such a nice man, and quite a gentleman."

"You knew him?" I shouldn't have been too surprised. Mona spent much of her time at the library. Even though Dawson appeared to be intensely private, it didn't mean she hadn't considered him a friend. "I'm sorry, I didn't realize that."

Mona nodded. "I was as good a friend as I could be to Dawson, anyway. You know he was someone who kept to himself. Sort of like Linus. Anyway, I thought Dawson was behaving peculiarly shortly before he stopped coming to the library."

"Peculiarly? In what way?"

Mona said, "Well, for a bit, I thought he was acting paranoid. He behaved as if he thought someone was peering over his shoulder, looking at what he was typing or researching. Dawson was jumpy. I came up from behind him when he was working and startled him so much, he nearly fell out of his chair."

I frowned. "That does seem like a change. I don't think I'd ever seen Dawson behaving that way."

"Exactly. Dawson quickly turned over pages he was looking at, too. It was just so very odd. I figured maybe they were his personal financial documents or something. It's the only thing I could understand that would make him act that way."

I looked back up at the shelf where Mona had been reaching when I walked up. Fitz had jumped up there. It was pretty common for the cat to get on a top shelf to get a better vantage point, but he seemed to nose around in the area where Mona had been trying to reach.

"See?" she asked. "Fitz thinks there's something up there, too. Dawson wasn't putting things on the shelf after I startled him, but I was keeping an eye on him when I returned to my knitting. Someone walked inside the library, and then I spotted Dawson messing around on the top shelf."

"You saw him putting some of his papers there?"

Mona shrugged. "I don't know what he put up there, but I noticed he didn't have as many papers on the table in front of him as he had before reaching up there."

I was taller than Mona and had no problem gently pushing books aside to pull out some papers that had been hidden between them.

"What are they?" breathed Mona.

It was what I was trying to figure out, myself. Dawson seemed to use his own type of shorthand. Plus, his handwriting was difficult to decipher. I said slowly, "I think these are notes about something he was investigating for a newspaper story. I'd have to spend more time studying them, though."

Mona sounded relieved. "I'm glad you have them, Ann. I was going to fret until they were in safe hands. The funny thing is, I'd put Dawson's odd behavior totally out of my mind. Then, when Luna told me what happened to him, I was simply in so much shock that I didn't think more about the papers or Dawson's behavior. Until this morning, that is."

"Thanks for letting me know. Can you describe the person who came into the library? The one who startled Dawson into putting the papers in a hidden spot?"

Mona squinted her eyes and furrowed her brow, trying to dredge up the memory. Then she gave a regretful shake of her head. "I don't seem to remember. I can't even remember if they were male or female. I was more interested in what Dawson was doing. I'm sorry, Ann."

"Don't be sorry at all. You've been a tremendous help. Just let me know if you happen to notice this person in the library again."

"Will do," she said. For a second, I thought she might salute. Somehow, I had the feeling I'd deputized Mona.

"Want to come down, Fitz? You were helpful, too," I said.

Fitz looked proud of himself and perhaps just the slightest bit smug. Then he bounded down from the shelf.

Back home that evening, I spread the papers out on my kitchen table while Fitz lay curled in my lap. I stared down at Dawson's notes, which I'd spent some time decrypting. *Old logs don't match the stories. Need to cross-reference dates and times. Someone's been careful all these years.*

I scanned further down the page: *Watching and waiting. People talk more when they think no one's paying attention.*

It definitely seemed Dawson was onto something. It was equally obvious that he was being careful not to reveal what it was. At this point, though, my eyes were growing heavy, and the words were blurring together on the page.

"What do you think, Fitz?" I asked, scratching the soft fur behind his ears. He responded with a sleepy, rattling purr that seemed to indicate he thought it was time to turn in. The papers would still be there in the morning.

Chapter Thirteen

I woke up the next morning when my phone pinged to let me know I'd gotten a text. I sleepily rolled over and grabbed it. It was Grayson. Instead of trying to text when I was half-asleep, I called him instead.

"Ah, sorry. I woke you up," said Grayson regretfully.

"No, it's fine. I needed to get up, anyway. But you sound like you've been up for hours."

Grayson said, "I'm not sure I ever fell really properly to sleep. But I've been amped up on caffeine for the last few hours, so I've got lots of energy. Whether or not I'll be able to sustain it the rest of the day is another story. Anyway, want to grab breakfast together? My treat. I'm sorry I haven't been around lately."

Grayson and I had been talking about moving in together, but whenever it seemed it would happen, life threw an obstacle or two our way. It was fine, the separate households, but it really did mean we didn't spend as much time together when things got busy.

"Breakfast would be great," I said. "How much time do you have this morning? Is your morning as crazy as yesterday?"

"I'm cautiously optimistic it won't be that bad. Is there something you wanted to do? A hike? Something like that?"

I said, "Actually, I think I'd like to check back in with Tessa Hayes. Maybe follow up on those financial irregularities we found?"

"The financial irregularities *you* found," said Grayson. "You deserve all the credit for that discovery. Sure, let's run by the county manager's office after we eat. I'll be by in a few minutes."

While waiting for Grayson, I figured I should give the county manager's office a quick call, just to make sure Tessa was in today. After all, her job probably entailed being out in the field at least some of the time. I was glad I phoned because they said she had a personal day off today. It just meant we'd need to drop by her house instead of her office. And that she might not be at home, either.

Breakfast was a treat. Quittin' Time, despite inadequacies in other respects, could make a fantastic Southern breakfast. We'd ordered pretty basic stuff last time, but went more elaborate this time around. I had a grits bowl topped with spinach, tomatoes, shrimp, and cheese. Grayson opted for a Greek omelet with hash browns on the side. Both of them were excellent, and the waitress came by regularly to top off our coffees until I was almost as caffeinated as Grayson was.

I caught up Grayson on my visit with Julie Hartwell at the gym the day before. Grayson listened intently while polishing off his food.

"What did you make of Julie's alibi?" he asked. "That book club meeting at the library."

"That book club is no alibi at all. It's a morning club. And it certainly doesn't last all day."

Grayson said, "I'm surprised Julie acknowledged her husband was having an affair with Rachel. And I'm a bit surprised they're still married."

"She was a little defensive about it, understandably. Of course, she was bitter about Rachel betraying their friendship. Julie was more helpful when she was talking about Andrew Campbell and why he might be a better suspect."

Grayson smiled, "I gathered that when you said she called Andrew 'the merry widower.'"

"Yeah, she doesn't seem to think much of him, that's for sure."

"Speaking of getting caught up," I said, "I should tell you what Mona and Fitz helped me find at the library yesterday. There were some notes Dawson had hidden on a top shelf in nonfiction."

Grayson paused, with his fork halfway to his mouth. "Hidden notes? What did they say?"

I told him about the cryptic entries, comparing records and mentioning someone watching and waiting. "Dawson wrote that people talk more when they think no one's paying attention."

"Sounds like he was piecing something together," said Grayson thoughtfully. "Did Mona see who might have spooked him into hiding the notes?"

"She couldn't remember. But she said Dawson had been jumpy near the end. Maybe he realized he was in danger or was getting close to finding out the truth."

The waitress came by with the bill, and Grayson quickly paid it. "To the town hall?" he asked.

"I forgot to mention Tessa took a personal day today. Want to check her house first and see if she's there? I have the photos of the documents in question on my phone."

Grayson said, "Perfect. Sure, let's see if we can beard the lion in her den."

I looked up Tessa's address and directed us over there. It was a stately Colonial with crisp white paint and black shutters. A brick pathway wound through an immaculately maintained front yard, dormant now in February, but still showing signs of careful planning in its structured layout.

"Nice place," said Grayson. "And Tessa's car is in the driveway. That's promising."

We walked over to the front door and rang the doorbell. We waited a few moments, and no one answered.

Grayson reached out to knock loudly on the front door. No response to that approach, either.

"Maybe she's in the shower or something," he said with a frown. "We could try to come back later."

I turned to look again at the pristine yard. "Do you think she might be around back? Considering it's February, it's really a warm day, especially in the sun. It looks like Tessa might be a yard person. Maybe she'd want to work outside on a day off."

"Good idea," said Grayson, and followed me toward the backyard.

Even in winter, the space showed Tessa's precise nature—bare rose canes carefully pruned and tied to winter trellises, surrounded by geometrically perfect boxwood hedges. The morning frost sparkled on the gravel paths beside the beds.

"No sign of her," said Grayson.

But I'd frozen. "Look there," I pointed. There was a boot peeking out from the bottom of a boxwood.

We hurried around to find Tessa Hayes crumpled beside a dormant rose brush. She was wearing a winter coat over what looked like gardening clothes. Rusty garden shears, their blades stained crimson, were discarded among the roses.

Chapter Fourteen

The next few minutes felt like a blur. Grayson carefully checked for a pulse while I dialed Burton with shaking fingers. I quickly gave Burton the basic information as Grayson stood, face pale, and shook his head.

"Grayson says there's no pulse," I said, my voice as shaky as my hands had been.

"On my way," said Burton in a clipped voice.

Grayson and I walked carefully back to Grayson's car. We sat with the heat running and kept an eye to make sure no one came up to disturb what was clearly a crime scene. Soon Burton and the state police arrived with blue lights and sirens. I pointed to the backyard, and they quickly headed in that direction. Minutes later, crime scene tape was being strung up by grim officers.

Burton walked over to the car, and we stepped out. He gave us a tired look. "Seems like we just went through this, you and I. How are you two doing?"

I glanced at Grayson. "We're holding up."

"Did you have any idea that Tessa was in any sort of danger?" asked Burton.

"No," said Grayson. "And she didn't realize we were coming over this morning. Ann had a few follow-up questions about the financial irregularities she'd spotted in the documents she'd reviewed."

Burton raised an eyebrow. "You didn't try to find her at work? It's a workday, after all."

"I called her office, and they told me she'd taken a personal day today," I explained. "So we decided to drop by her house. We didn't call ahead." For a good reason. I'd thought if we'd called ahead, Tessa might not have wanted to talk with us at all.

Burton nodded. "Okay. You've both done some good work on the cold case side. But you're obviously getting really close to something the murderer wants to keep secret. This is the second body you've discovered in the last week."

Grayson nodded. "We'll be careful."

I said, "Do you think this will make a difference in terms of whether the state police or your department start looking into the cold case?"

Burton sighed. "Who knows? I'd certainly think so, but the state police are definitely the ones running the show. The fact of the matter is, though, two murders in a town this size? There's most likely a connection. It would be very unusual for two different murderers to be on the loose in a place like Whitby. That's going to mean some reviewing."

Someone called out to Burton. "I've gotta go," he said. "You two watch your steps."

Grayson carefully drove away, and we were silent for a couple of minutes. "It's unbelievable," said Grayson.

"I know. Do you think that someone was trying to keep Tessa from spilling the beans about anything illegal that was going on with these different transactions?"

"It could be," I said slowly. "Or maybe Tessa knew something about Dawson's murder."

"Did you get that impression?" asked Grayson.

I said, "I felt like Tessa was very experienced working in the public eye. She seemed to be more in PR mode to me. You know: 'nothing to see here.'"

"Yeah, that's what I thought too," said Grayson. "She seemed to be interested in covering her bases and making sure she was being totally transparent."

"But maybe she was so used to putting on a public face that she could hide what she knew."

We drove on for a little while and were passing the botanical gardens when Grayson started slowing the car down. "Well, would you look at that. Ethan's car."

Sure enough, it was a luxury car that I'd recognized from outside Ethan's office the last time we talked to him. One of those tremendous SUVs with all the extra options. There really wasn't another vehicle in the small town of Whitby that was similar. Big vehicles in Whitby usually equated pickup trucks.

"Thinking we should take a stroll in the botanical gardens?" I asked, quirking an eyebrow. "It's a shame I don't have Ivy with me."

"Sure," said Grayson lightly. "After all, February is a great time of year to visit."

I chuckled at that. "Actually, the greenhouses will be worth a look, if we want to stroll through them. Other than that, it might look a little barren."

But there was a lot more life in the gardens than I'd expected. There were witch hazel trees in full bloom, their spidery yellow flowers bright against the bare branches. Red-twig dogwoods provided some striking color, too. And I spotted winter jasmine trailing yellow blooms over stone walls. My great-aunt had been quite a gardener and had taught me that every season had its wonders. Paths and walkways snaked across the grounds, dormant fountains were draped with protective covers, and stone benches were scattered throughout.

"Now it's just a matter of finding Ethan," I said.

"Not an easy task. This place is pretty big."

"Let's shoot for the greenhouse," I said.

The greenhouse rose from the grounds like a Victorian crystal palace, its glass panels frosted with the morning chill. Inside, though, it felt tropical in comparison and the humid warmth fogged the windows. I spotted orchids and exotic-looking ferns. There were also cacti and succulents of all sorts under bright grow lights.

And there was Ethan. He was strolling through the greenhouse, his crisp black wool overcoat and leather gloves a stark contrast to the natural setting. He didn't seem to be looking at the plants, really, but appeared to be deep in his own thoughts. Until he spotted us, of course.

"Well," he said with a frown. "Fancy meeting you two here." He seemed to try to act casual, but there was still an edge to his voice.

"Yes," said Grayson in a cheerful voice. "Ann and I thought we'd take in the garden. I've only been here a couple of times, and she's something of a regular."

If being a regular meant coming twice a year, I supposed I qualified. I gave Ethan a tight smile.

"It's a beautiful place," said Ethan briskly. "I like to come over to clear my head."

I nodded. "It's another reason Grayson and I are here. We've had a pretty rough morning."

Ethan gave me a polite smile. "That sounds ominous. Traffic on the roads? Car trouble, perhaps?"

"We found Tessa Hayes dead this morning," I said flatly, watching Ethan closely for a reaction.

I couldn't quite read his response, though, because it was quickly masked by a concerned frown. "You can't be serious," he said. "Are you saying Tessa had some sort of latent health issue that suddenly popped to the forefront?"

Grayson shook his head. "We're not saying anything like that, unfortunately. And we're most definitely serious. She was murdered. The police are with her now."

Ethan looked away. "Shocking news. Tessa was an exemplary and dedicated public servant."

"Have you been here all morning, then?" asked Grayson, still in that friendly tone.

Ethan turned to look back at Grayson. "I was at an early business meeting. Like I said, I came here to clear my mind. You're not insinuating anything, are you?"

"Of course not," said Grayson mildly. "I was just making conversation."

"I haven't seen Tessa for a while, you understand. Our paths don't always cross when it comes to work. Also, she's been very busy, so an email usually suffices instead of an in-person visit. It's quicker for both parties. We're both inundated with meetings, so it's nice to avoid them whenever possible."

This qualified as a speech from Ethan, who'd kept his replies fairly short to us. But somehow, I got the feeling he wasn't telling the complete truth. For one thing, he was fidgeting with his leather gloves, and he didn't seem much of a fidgeter. He was also not looking at Grayson or me very often.

"It's a shame we didn't get the chance to speak with Tessa," I said. "We wanted to learn more about the irregularities we found in the paperwork from her office."

Ethan stiffened. "I know nothing about that. And you probably don't really know much, either. These business documents can be very complex. There might have been sections of the accounting that simply went over your head."

As a research librarian, I didn't particularly appreciate the inference that I didn't know what I was looking at. But I nodded. "Sure." I enjoyed the sympathetic eye-roll Grayson gave me.

I continued, "Last time, you mentioned Andrew Campbell as a potential suspect for Rachel's death. And Dawson's."

Now it was Ethan's turn to roll his eyes. "I'd like it to go on the record that I have absolutely no idea who murdered Dawson Blake, since I really didn't know the man. But yes, I believe Rachel's husband to be a conceivable suspect in his wife's death. Statistics show spouses are the most likely candidates, anyway."

Grayson pushed, "And you have no other thoughts about who could have murdered Rachel?"

Ethan opened his mouth to issue his standard denial, then paused. He said, "There was one other item of note. A couple of years ago, I was at a funeral service. While there, I noticed a man not far away, lingering at a grave. He looked quite distraught."

"Was it someone you recognized?" I asked.

"It was Calvin Mercer," said Ethan with a small shrug. "He's a woodworker. Actually, he does fine work. I've had him over at my home in the past, creating built-in cabinetry. He's quite an artisan."

Calvin Mercer's work, I suspected, was a bit out of my price range. But I nodded, encouraging Ethan to continue.

Which he did. "At the end of the service I was attending, I took a quick detour to see the grave where Calvin had been lingering. It was Rachel Campbell's. He'd left a single rose there." Ethan waited for a few moments to let what he was saying sink in. "I found that rather significant, as was his manner. He'd looked like a man who was nursing old wounds."

Then Ethan said briskly, "Now, I must be on my way. It's time for me to head to the office."

We watched him stride out. "It's interesting that he has a tear in his coat sleeve. Ethan's so immaculately dressed, otherwise."

Grayson raised an eyebrow at me. "That *is* interesting. You've got sharp eyes."

"For inconsistencies, at any rate."

Grayson said regretfully, "I guess I should be going to the office, too. See if I can reassign some of these stories to other staff."

"And I should walk Ivy again."

Grayson asked, "How are things going with her?"

"She's such a good girl," I said. "She and Fitz seem to like each other just fine. And she hasn't been mopey about Linus at all."

We got into Grayson's car. "Shouldn't Linus be getting home?"

"That's right. He's called a few times to check on her, and I told him everything was great. He decided to extend his stay just a smidge, but he'll be back later today."

Chapter Fifteen

Grayson dropped me off at home, then drove off for the newspaper office. I walked in to find Ivy and Fitz peacefully sharing a warm sunbeam on my kitchen floor. "Want to take a walk?" I asked Ivy gently.

But Ivy gave me an apologetic look. She was enjoying the sunbeam far too much for that. Instead, I set about doing a bit of housework before settling down with a book. Although I loved going to the library for an early shift, the days where I didn't go in until the afternoon were really just as nice.

Unfortunately, this idyll was interrupted by Zelda knocking on my door. She looked like a miniature virago with a cigarette. "It's happening again!" she practically shouted at me.

"What? What's happening?" I asked calmly. Although the entire sense of calm I'd felt just minutes ago had dissipated.

"The *boy*," hissed Zelda, looking at me as if I had suddenly become very slow. "The bad boy in the neighborhood. I was out walking Ivy just a few minutes ago, and he was out in the neighborhood again! Trying to break into cars and whatnot."

Well, that answered the mystery of why Ivy hadn't been interested in yet another walk. And perhaps why there was the faintest aroma of stale cigarette smoke in my home. "What do you want me to do, Zelda? Call Burton?" I felt guilty that I hadn't told him the last time.

"The police are simply too busy right now to handle this. They have murders and goodness knows what else. No, I'm going to take care of it. I know where the boy lives. I saw him coming out of the duplex apartment yesterday when I was driving back from work. And this morning," said Zelda triumphantly, "I saw his mother's car parked there. I *never* see a car there."

I did not think it was a good idea for Zelda to be ranting at the mother. All that would likely accomplish is getting her back up. "I'll go with you," I said.

"Whatever," said Zelda. "But I'm going now. Aren't you working today?" She gave me a look through narrowed eyes, as if suspecting I was playing hooky myself.

"This afternoon, just to fill in for someone who's leaving early. I have plenty of time."

Zelda gave a humph, but acquiesced, to my relief and stubbed out the dregs of her cigarette. Although it was a short drive to the duplex, Zelda was determined to drive and already had her car parked outside my house.

The duplex was an older one, made of red brick with window units. Zelda marched right up to the front door and pounded on it, making me wince. She was about to do it a second time when I said, "Hey, let's give her a chance to make it to the door first."

A few seconds later, the door slowly opened. A woman was standing there, dark circles shadowing her eyes as she gripped a chipped coffee mug. She was wearing what looked like a uniform from an overnight cleaning job. "Can I help you?" she asked uncertainly.

Zelda announced without preamble, "Your son has been trying to break into cars. During *school* hours. Playing hooky." She immediately started a coughing fit from some earlier cigarette.

"Zelda," I said quietly, shooting her a look. To the mother, I said as gently as I could, "We're concerned about your son. It seems like he might be having a tough time."

The woman suddenly just looked defeated, her shoulders slumping. "I didn't know he wasn't in school. I work nights cleaning offices and days in the grocery store." Her voice cracked at the end of the sentence.

Zelda gave her a skeptical look. "Nobody else can keep an eye on him?"

The woman raised her head up higher in a somewhat defensive posture. "His father left us. We lost the house, so now we're renting. And rent isn't cheap, you know? I can barely keep up. If he hasn't been at school, he's not getting his free breakfast and lunch, either."

Zelda narrowed her eyes. "But why isn't he in *school*? Does he just keep missing the bus?"

The woman sat wearily in a rickety kitchen chair. "I'm sleeping when the bus comes. I just get a few hours a day of sleep. I guess he hasn't been catching the bus on purpose." She rubbed her face. "Owen said he was being bullied."

"Bullied!" hissed Zelda. It was a voice that didn't bode well for any bullies Zelda happened across.

The woman nodded. "Yeah. We had to change schools when we lost the house. Changed towns, too, because I couldn't find a job where we were living. So he's the new kid. And he's small for his age, too." She sighed. "I don't know what to do. Nothing's going right. If I could, I'd take him out of the school, just to keep him from the bullies. But I don't have a lot of choices right now."

I said slowly, "Would you be interested in homeschooling? Unfortunately, the town is too small for other options."

The woman frowned at me as if I hadn't been listening very closely. "Well, I'm working at the grocery store during the day, like I was saying. Owen's dad isn't giving us any money, so if I don't work, we're not eating. And we're not eating much, as it is, especially if Owen is ditching school."

Zelda made another hissing sound. This one suggested Owen's dad should watch his back if he showed up in the neighborhood.

I said, "The reason I asked is because I'm a librarian at the Whitby Library. We have a homeschool collective that meets there. There are various moms and a couple of dads that cover the different subjects. It seems to be a pretty organized outfit. I just wondered if it might be a solution."

There was a flicker of interest in the woman's eyes. Then she said regretfully, "I wouldn't be able to drive him over to the library and back."

Zelda said with a humph, "I could help with that. Boy should be in school. Or homeschool, or whatever."

I quickly said, "I could ask among the other parents if anyone would like to come by to talk with you about it. Maybe they could drive him there, or Zelda could. See what you think." I thought of Timothy from film club, our volunteer teen for library tech days. He was also in the collective. Maybe either Timothy or his mother could carpool.

The woman said slowly, "I couldn't afford any fees is the problem."

"The library resources are free," I said quietly. "And the collective shares materials."

Zelda said fiercely, "I can help keep an eye on Owen. I volunteer in the library, shelving books. I can bring food for him, too, since cooking for one is just silly. Someone has to make sure these kids stay on the straight and narrow. We watch out for each other in this neighborhood." In a slight deviation from the topic, she said, "Did you know Mrs. Henderson still has Christmas lights up? I was telling Ann earlier. In February! The whole neighborhood's falling to pieces."

The mother gave a watery laugh, and I hid a smile. Under Zelda's bluster, there was genuine concern. Even if she had a tendency to express it by way of property values and HOA violations.

The woman gave us a shy look. "I'm Sarah Mitchell. Thanks for looking out for Owen."

Zelda and I gave her our phone numbers and full names, then we got hers. I promised Sarah I'd get back to her with more information soon. Zelda looked as if she might want to linger, perhaps to give the long-suffering Sarah more unwanted parenting advice.

"We should go let Sarah get some sleep before her shift at the store," I prompted Zelda. She looked for a moment like she might balk, but then muttered under her breath and followed me out of the duplex.

"She seemed like a very hard-working mom," I said, hoping Zelda was mollified and wouldn't be harassing the woman later on.

Zelda nodded in agreement, to my surprise. Her mind was already racing ahead to the next thing she was involved in. "Think I should walk Ivy again?"

I thought poor Ivy needed a break from Zelda's good intentions. "I think she'll be okay until Linus comes back later today. He's going to meet up with me after work to take her home."

"No reason for Linus to have to wait to reunite with Ivy," said Zelda firmly. "I'll text him to let him know I'll meet him at your house when he comes into town."

Which reminded me again I needed to get my house key back from Zelda. Apparently, though, after she was in my house one more time. "If it's no trouble," I said. "I'm sure Linus is ready to see her again."

I was able to successfully detach myself from Zelda by reminding her I needed to leave for the library. She quickly dispatched me, since she was never one to believe in shirking one's responsibilities.

Unfortunately, I walked into the library to find a state of chaos. My usually immaculate library director was standing in the middle of it, his shirt sleeves rolled up, suit jacket off, and tie askew. Wilson gave me a look of utter relief when he saw me. "Ann. Thank goodness you're here."

"What's going on with the printer?" I asked. Because it was always the printer. The printer's antics could take a completely normal day at the library and turn it completely on its head.

"I have no idea," said Wilson desperately. "It's lost its mind. Print jobs are disappearing, gibberish is being printed out. I know you're a wonder with the thing. Can you fix it?"

I was already moving toward the possessed machine. "We can't get the repair guy over here?"

"Stuck at another job," said Wilson. "It's been a nightmare. Patrons are being prompted for their document ID or password and of course, they don't have one." Wilson glanced back at his office with intense longing on his face.

I had mercy on him. Actually, the fact was that he was going to be absolutely no use with the printer and would wring his hands, which wouldn't help at all. "Why don't you just head back to your office and catch up on whatever you were working on."

Wilson's relieved expression came back again. "Do you have any thoughts on what might be the problem?"

"My thought is that it's the twenty-year-old printer software program. We're sure we don't have any room in this year's budget to upgrade our printer? If it's acting up in February, the outlook for the rest of the year isn't wonderful."

The only way to really pressure Wilson over improvements was when you had him over a barrel. As was the current situation.

Wilson frowned. "I'd have to review the budget to see if we could squeeze something out." He paused, looking at the patrons standing around the dysfunctional machine-like mourners at a funeral. One was frantically refreshing her email for missing documents, another was muttering about paying taxes that covered my salary, and a third insisted that surely we could retrieve his files from "the queue."

"I'll see what I can do," I said.

After about forty-five minutes, I cowed the printer into submission. Relieved patrons swamped it like Black Friday shoppers, waiting to print whatever documents they needed. I slipped away back to the circulation desk, which was what I was supposed to cover for my absent colleague.

Luna sidled up to me with a grin on her face.

"You're some kind of printer genius," she said.

"More like I've had a lot of practice," I said wryly. "I've been here long enough that I know all its quirks and foibles."

Luna lowered her voice. "You know Wilson's in there right now, on the phone with someone about the budget. I heard him say something about 'critical infrastructure needs.'"

I smiled. Sometimes Wilson's fastidiousness worked in our favor. He hated anything in the library looking less than perfect; which meant the ancient printer's rebellion might finally get us the upgrade we desperately needed.

"Though if we do get a new printer," Luna added thoughtfully, "what will Wilson do with all the time he usually spends hiding in his office during printer emergencies?"

"I'm sure he'll find something," I said. "There's always the Wi-Fi to worry about."

Luna laughed and headed back to the children's section, leaving me to help a patron who was eyeing the printer with clear suspicion. I didn't blame them one bit.

I checked out a few books and helped some patrons who were looking for help in the stacks. Then I noticed Calvin Mercer at a table not far from the periodicals. His salt-and-pepper hair was falling over his forehead as he sketched something in a notebook.

"Calvin?" I asked hesitantly.

He startled a little, then smiled as he spotted me. "Hi there, Ann. I wondered if I might see you here today."

"Getting some work done?"

Calvin chuckled. "If you can call it that. I have a client who wants me to make a reproduction of a period piece. It seems a lot easier than it is."

"It doesn't seem easy at all to me," I said wryly. "What type of furniture is it?"

"A Chippendale highboy with intricate carvings." Calvin gestured to a pile of woodworking magazines he'd pulled out. "I wanted to take a look at your archives to get ideas. It's going to take forever for me to make this thing."

"I hope you're being paid handsomely for it."

Calvin gave me a grin. "Yeah, the pay isn't going to be a problem." He nodded with his head to indicate the printer. "Looks like you were able to subdue the printer over there."

"After some wrangling," I said. "I hope you weren't disturbed by all the commotion."

"Not a bit. One reason I like coming to the library is I get too distracted at the shop sometimes. Here, I know that any commotion or issues have nothing to do with me, so it's easier to focus." He paused. "How are things going with you and Grayson and the investigative piece you're doing for the paper? Any good leads?"

I hesitated. But one thing I knew about Whitby is that news traveled fast. And Burton and the state police hadn't yet switched over to work the cold case connection to Dawson Blake's death. "Unfortunately, I have some bad news. Tessa Hayes is dead. Grayson and I found her this morning. It appears to be murder."

Calvin's eyes grew wide. "No."

"I'm afraid so."

Calvin started shoving papers into his worn leather portfolio, his movements jerky and rushed. "I shouldn't be talking about this. Tessa *and* Dawson? It's got to be because of something they knew. And I don't know anything, Ann."

I said quietly, "I think you're safe. Dawson was actively investigating Rachel's death and Tessa was someone with lots of fingers in lots of pies. But I understand if you don't want to talk about it all. I'm just trying to help get to the bottom of things before anyone else gets hurt."

Calvin stopped his frenetic paper stuffing, sitting back in his chair. He asked in a low voice, "It was definitely murder?"

"I'm afraid so." I stopped for a few moments. "Calvin, I don't think you were totally honest with me about not knowing Dawson Blake."

He avoided looking at me. "I told you he took photos at different craft fairs I attended."

"Yes, but you made it sound as if you two really weren't acquainted. And I just don't think that's so." I made it sound as if I knew something, but the truth was, it was more that everyone knew everybody in Whitby. It seemed odd to me that Calvin and Dawson wouldn't have run in some of the same circles.

I gestured to one sketch that he hadn't grabbed yet. "One thing I've noticed about you is how precise and controlled you are with your work. I guess that must be an important trait in a woodworker. You have to make careful measurements and pay attention to detail. You're in control of your measurements, your designs, and the narrative you tell."

Calvin's eyes were guarded. "I'm not sure what you mean. About controlling a narrative."

"Well, when we first talked with you about Dawson, you had your story all mapped out. He was the guy who covered the craft fairs for the paper—nothing more. But that wasn't the whole picture, was it?"

I could tell Calvin was feeling like he wanted to bolt again as he glanced toward the exit.

I continued, "You even had an alibi before anybody asked for one. All the details laid out, just so."

"Because I had nothing to hide." Calvin's voice, however, lacked conviction. He sighed, then finally made eye contact with me. "Look. I don't want to get involved in this. Like I mentioned before, I think investigating this stuff is dangerous. I'll tell you what I know, then I want you to keep away from me."

I nodded, waiting for him to continue.

He nervously moistened his lips. "Dawson came to talk to me because of the grants. He'd figured out I spent a lot of time in the county manager's office, getting grants of my own for woodworking."

"What kinds of questions was he asking?"

Calvin rubbed his face with his hands. "He was asking questions about what I might have picked up at the county manager's office."

I frowned. "But your grants were obviously very different from the commercial grants that Dawson would have been looking into."

"Sure. But have you spent much time in the county manager's office in town hall? The walls are as thin as carbon copies. You can hear anything anybody was saying in there. And I spent a lot of time sitting around, cooling my heels, waiting to talk with somebody about my own, piddly craft grants. The developers always went first."

I said slowly, "So you overheard a lot of sensitive information."

Calvin shrugged. "I overheard enough to make Dawson happy, apparently. He'd ask how money was distributed and which contractors got picked. Dawson swore me to secrecy. He thought he was really close to a big story about where money was really going. Taxpayer money, you understand. Then Dawson is murdered. Now Tessa is murdered. Sure seems like a cover-up to me. You can see why I'm spooked."

"Did Dawson share with you what he'd learned?"

"No." Calvin started gathering his things again, more slowly this time. "But the day before his death, he told me he had proof. He was going to meet with someone to verify it. I told him not to go. It sounded dangerous to me."

I wondered if the person who was verifying information was the same person who'd killed him in the abandoned warehouse. I felt a shiver go up my spine.

I said, "You definitely got the impression that what Dawson was focused on was a potential financial scandal at town hall. There was nothing else?"

Calvin shook his head.

I nodded. "Where were you this morning? When Tessa died?"

Calvin gave me a wry look. "So now I'm killing county managers?"

"I'm just asking what the police would ask if they start looking in this direction."

Calvin sighed. "I was having breakfast at Quittin' Time. I go there every morning for coffee and a meal before heading into my shop. But I don't have any reason to kill Tessa. Nor Dawson. And definitely not Rachel. So it doesn't make any sense that I'd be a suspect in any way."

But if Rachel had rejected Calvin, might he have lashed out at her? Maybe my thoughts were reflected on my face because Calvin said, "I totally accepted Rachel's decision to stay with Andrew. It disappointed me, but I accepted it. I'm not an unreasonable person. I wasn't going to kill someone I loved simply because she didn't love me back."

"What did you make of Tessa?"

Calvin considered this. "She was dedicated to the town. Tessa was a hard worker—the kind of person who was at work early and left late." He frowned. "Wait, where was Tessa's body found? At the office?"

"At home."

His frown deepened. "Really? So she was killed last night?"

"Apparently, it was this morning."

Calvin shook his head. "That just doesn't make any sense. Today's a work day. Why wasn't Tessa at work? She was always at work."

"I was told Tessa took today off for personal reasons."

Calvin looked spooked again. "It's just seriously odd. I guess Tessa was trying to de-stress? Maybe she was trying to think through what was going on with Dawson's death? Or those financial irregularities. Then somebody saw their chance and took her out. After all, Tessa would be a tough person to murder. Killing someone at the town hall would be a difficult proposition. There's security going into the building."

I hadn't thought of that, but it made sense. Maybe the killer had staked Tessa out, waiting for the opportunity to murder her. I felt that shiver up my spine again.

I asked, "Last time I spoke with you, you mentioned Julie Hartwell being a suspect for Rachel's death. Do you still feel that way?"

Calvin blew his breath out into a sigh. "I suppose so. Although it's easier for me to picture her murdering Rachel than it is Dawson and Tessa." He mulled this over for a few moments. "Maybe she felt Dawson and Tessa knew too much about Rachel's death and decided she had to silence them." He cast another worried glance around the library. "Sorry, but I'd really like to get out of here."

"Of course. I'll put away the magazines, if you'd like."

Calvin said wryly, "I'd been planning on copying the articles on the all-in-one printer, but it's looking a little crazy over there."

Sure enough, the line at the printer hadn't improved. I could only hope that it wasn't because the thing was on the fritz again.

"I could always copy the articles later and keep the copies up front for you at the reference desk."

Calvin gave me a genuine smile at that. "Would you? That would be great. I can run by tomorrow and grab them, for sure. I've got the magazines open to the articles I need. Thanks, Ann, you're a lifesaver." With that, he quickly headed out.

Chapter Sixteen

The printer fortunately behaved itself the rest of the day. I busied myself with patron requests and social media scheduling for the library. Then I saw Timothy coming in with his mom. It wasn't at all unusual seeing Timothy come into the library, but since he could drive, it wasn't as often that his mother accompanied him.

I waved to them, and they came right over. Timothy grinned at me. "You look relieved. Are you needing us to have another library tech day?"

"Well, actually, *yes*. There have been a lot of patrons lately whose phones are mysteries to them. But as a matter of fact, it was your mom I needed to ask a favor of this time."

Timothy's mother was a pleasant-looking woman in her mid-forties with graying brown hair. Christine laughed. "I hope it's not about technology. Timothy manages all our tech at home. When he leaves for college, it's going to be revealed to the world that we're total Luddites."

"No, not about tech, fortunately," I said. "I wanted to ask you about a family who's interested in the homeschool collective." I filled her in on Owen, his background, the challenges the family was facing, and homeschooling as an alternative to the issues Owen was dealing with.

"The main problem," I said, "is that Owen's mom has a tough work schedule and can't really get him to the library for the collective."

But before I even finished the sentence, she was already cutting me off. "I'd be delighted to drive him to the library and back."

I smiled at her. "I haven't even told you where he lives. It might not be convenient for you."

Timothy said earnestly, "If it's not convenient for Mom, I can drive Owen. I mean, if it's okay with his mom and everything."

But Christine apparently thought that Timothy didn't really need to have young passengers in the car with him. "It's no bother at all. Whitby is only so big. It's not as if any house in town is going to be a long drive."

I nodded. "Perfect. How about if I set up a meeting between the two of you and Owen and his mother at the library? That way you can meet up and explain more about how the collective works and whether it might be a good fit for Owen."

Christine and Owen thought this was a fine idea, so I called Sarah Mitchell, intending on leaving a message for her. But she picked up as soon as I called.

"I'm sorry," I said. "I hope I'm not interrupting you at work."

"It's my day off from the grocery store. And I couldn't sleep, thinking about Owen. He's not at home and he's not at school. So where is he?" Sarah sounded exhausted and worried.

I told her why I was calling. She quickly said, "And they're at the library now? Christine and Timothy? I'm going to drive around, find Owen and bring him to the library. I've got to do something about this now."

Sarah got off the phone to drive, and I looked apologetically at Christine and Timothy. "I hope you're okay with having a meeting right now. Or as soon as Sarah can get her hands on Owen."

It seemed to be fine with them both, which was a good thing since I was called away by a patron and didn't have the chance to make more phone calls. Thirty minutes later, I saw Sarah coming into the library with a boy I took to be Owen. He was indeed a smaller boy with eyes that somehow managed to be wistful and somewhat defiant at the same time. His arms were folded across his chest.

Timothy, who was something of an old soul, reached out a hand to Owen. "Hi, Owen. I'm Timothy."

Owen regarded his hand with suspicion for a minute, as if it was some sort of terrible practical joke. Then, slowly, he reached out his own hand, briefly shaking it before quickly retracting it again.

Christine introduced herself to Owen and Sarah, then they walked off together on a quick tour of the library and a talk about the collective. Owen still had a wary expression on his face, but seemed to be slowly loosening up. Owen's mom looked hopeful for the first time since I'd met her.

The next morning, I rose early to get ready to head to the gym with Grayson. His schedule had been so tough lately that I felt I hadn't seen him nearly as much as usual. We really did need to combine households, no matter how much trouble that seemed like it would be.

Grayson picked me up with a smile on his face. "Good morning."

"Hello there," I said, grinning back at him as I stuffed my house key into the small pocket of my workout pants. "Feel like exercising?"

Grayson said in a rueful voice, "I really felt like rolling over and going back to sleep."

"But you're here now. That's something, isn't it? You managed to pull yourself out of bed and get ready."

Grayson snorted. "I guess I have to take my wins where I can lately." He looked over at me. "What have I missed? I feel like I've been totally out of the loop lately."

"Are things getting better at work? Or is it still crazy?"

Grayson said, "Oh, it's still crazy all right. But hopefully things might be working out. My staff is back in the office, for one thing. So there's improvement on the horizon. I'm assigning stuff that I've been handling back over to them. I'm hoping I can get everything back to normal soon and have more time to myself." He glanced over at me quickly before looking back at the road again. "A little more time for *us*."

"That'll be nice," I said, reaching out to squeeze his hand briefly.

The gym parking lot was full when we arrived, and Grayson had to make a couple of laps to find a space.

"Starting out with cardio?" asked Grayson, since that was usually my routine when I was with him.

"That sounds good," I said, following him inside. As we walked through the lobby, we passed a young couple arguing over their gym schedules and who needed to be home when.

"And that's why we need to figure out the whole living situation," Grayson said quietly, nodding toward them.

"It would make things easier," I agreed. "No more driving back and forth between houses just to feed Fitz or grab clean clothes."

"No more wondering whose turn it is to cook or who has the better coffee maker." He made a face. "Though mine just died this morning, so yours wins by default."

"Once all this is over," I said, "and once we figure out what happened to Rachel, Dawson and Tessa, maybe we should stop talking about moving in together and actually do it."

Grayson nodded, his expression growing serious. "Maybe we should."

I looked at my watch. It was actually about the time that Julie Hartwell should be getting out of her exercise class again. "Would you like to talk to Julie real quick before we work out? Her class should be wrapping up."

Grayson grinned at me. "I sense an ulterior motive for being at the gym."

"Most definitely. Although working out is also a priority, of course." I shrugged. "I've never been big on the classes, though. I like the small weight room and the small exercise machine room too much."

Grayson said, "Is there an unawkward way to approach her without making it look like you and I are lying in wait?"

"The last time I saw Julie, she was grabbing a drink before she returned home. We could hang out in the cafe for a few minutes."

We'd just sat down with our drinks when Julie came over, glowing with perspiration. "Well, hey there," she said, giving me a smile and looking curiously at Grayson.

I introduced Grayson to her. "Can I join you two after I get my smoothie? I had a question for you, Ann."

We nodded, and she came back a few minutes later with a bright orange drink. I asked her how her class was, and she talked enthusiastically about it for several minutes. Then, rather abruptly, she segued to: "I heard you found Tessa Hayes, Ann."

"I was actually with Grayson when we found her."

Julie's face became even more animated. "What is happening? I know Rachel worked for Tessa. Is this all something to do with the county manager's office?"

I shook my head. "We really don't know yet. It could be. Or it could be a completely different angle." I gestured to Grayson. "Grayson is the editor of the paper, and we're taking a little time to look into things."

Now Julie looked a little wary, and I wondered if I should have said anything. "The newspaper?"

Grayson quickly said, "Of course our conversation is off-the-record."

Julie relaxed. "Okay, good. I don't need to have quotes in the paper. But I do want to sort of talk it out. You're thinking these deaths are all related—Rachel's, Dawson's, and Tessa's? I mean, the community is at risk, right?"

That was a bit of a stretch, but Grayson and I nodded. Grayson said, "We're hoping you have some insights or know something that can help us."

She shifted in her seat for a moment. Then she said, "I didn't know Tessa personally, of course. Just that she was an elected official."

Tessa wasn't, actually. She'd been appointed by the local government. But that was beside the point.

"I mean, I don't follow local politics at all, so I never paid attention one way or another. But I bet she had enemies because of her political career, right?"

I said slowly, "That could be."

"You're thinking they're all connected, though, like I just said. So it all goes back to Rachel's death, doesn't it?"

Grayson said, "It seems like it could. We're trying to explore that possibility."

I said, "The last time I spoke to you, it seemed like you thought Andrew Campbell might have had something to do with Rachel's death."

"He's the most-likely suspect," said Julie with a shrug. "Why he would have killed Dawson and Tessa is what confuses me, though. I guess maybe Andrew would have murdered them if they knew he was guilty."

Grayson said gently, "I bet you're thinking more about Rachel's death since these other deaths have happened. That's only natural. Is there anything that maybe you'd forgotten about from ten years ago that suddenly has come to mind?"

Julie took a long sip of her smoothie, looking conflicted. Then she slowly said, "I might know something. But it doesn't mean anything. It's one of those pieces of information that could misdirect everybody and waste time."

I said, "I don't mind being misdirected."

"Me either," said Grayson. "And if it's been on your mind, maybe it's time to say something."

"Okay," said Julie. She tapped her perfectly manicured nails against her cup. "I wasn't going to say anything, but now Tessa's died. It seems like things are getting out of control." She took a deep breath. "The day Rachel died, I wasn't actually at book club the whole time like I told you before. I mean, I *was* there, but then I left a little early. I wasn't in the mood for a group, I guess. After I left, I spotted Wade's car."

"Wade?" I asked. "But he was out of town the day Rachel died."

Julie gave me a weary look. "He was supposed to be, sure. But his car was parked in front of Rachel and Andrew's house."

Grayson said, "Did you go inside?"

"Are you kidding? I didn't want to confront them like that. I went on home and ate a huge container of ice cream. Of course, he was supposed to be out of town, so he didn't come back home after that. So I drove back by Rachel's house again that afternoon. Wade's car was gone by that point."

"Then you heard about Rachel's death," I said quietly.

"Exactly. Of course, I didn't hear until the next morning, which is when the divers found her."

"Did you confront Wade about it?" I asked.

"No, I was afraid to. Wade has a temper sometimes. Not violent," she added quickly. "Just intense. And I didn't want to admit that I was basically stalking him that day."

I leaned forward. "Julie, if Wade wasn't really out of town that day—"

"I know what you're thinking," she interrupted. "But Wade didn't kill Rachel. Of that I'm sure. And he wouldn't have murdered Dawson or Tessa or *anybody*. He's just not capable of that." Julie's voice had taken on a defensive edge.

"Then why tell us now?" asked Grayson gently. "If you're sure Wade wasn't involved."

Julie gathered her gym bag, standing abruptly. "Because somebody needs to know the truth about that day, and I've kept it bottled up too long inside me. I feel like I'm corroding from the inside with that secret."

Before we could ask her more questions, she hurried away, leaving her half-finished orange smoothie on the table.

Chapter Seventeen

"Well," said Grayson after a moment. "That was interesting."

"Very. Especially since Wade's alibi for Rachel's death just fell apart. He wasn't out of town, at all. Maybe Rachel wanted to end her affair with Wade and he lashed out at her. Maybe we should talk with him."

Grayson nodded. "Absolutely. Let's add him to the list of folks to speak to."

We got rid of our trash and headed over to the main gym area. Grayson said, "I'm already starving, and I haven't even started working out. Want to go to Quittin' Time after this? I'll probably have about an hour after we exercise before I need to head over to the office."

"Sounds good to me. That means we can also check Calvin's alibi for Tessa's murder. That's where he was supposed to be when Tessa died. He told me he goes there every morning for coffee and a meal before heading into his workshop."

I tried to give my workout my full focus, but I kept getting distracted by thoughts about the murders. I lost count when doing kettle ball lifts and had to start over. Finally, I got on the treadmill, figuring I was going to continue being pretty hopeless at the other parts of my workout. After running for about twenty minutes, I saw Grayson smiling sheepishly at me from the door. I stopped the treadmill.

"Everything okay?" I asked.

"Yeah, everything is fine except my brain apparently. I can't seem to keep my mind on what I'm doing. I think I'm going to give up."

I grinned at him. "Oh, that's too funny. I had the same problem. Maybe it means you and I are coming close to figuring things out. Our minds are trying to sort through the details and come up with the solution."

"I guess. I just wish I could stop my brain sometimes. I really needed that workout."

I said, "I think chasing down leads counts as cardio, right?"

"Something like that," said Grayson with a chuckle.

The familiar scent of coffee and biscuits greeted us as we walked into the restaurant. Since it was mid-morning by now, the breakfast rush had died down, leaving only a few regulars scattered around, cupping their coffee mugs in their hands.

Heather, who was our regular waitress, came over with a pot of coffee as we slid into a booth. "The usual for you two?" she asked, filling our cups. "Or are you having the basic breakfast like you do the days you're not as hungry?"

We were apparently quite predictable. Grayson and I had begun eating here fairly often after working out, with Grayson footing the bills. "That's right," said Grayson, grinning at her. "A Greek omelet and hash browns for me."

"And I'll have the grits bowl with spinach, tomatoes, and cheese," I said.

As Heather jotted down our order, I asked casually, "Hey, Grayson and I were hoping to catch up with Calvin Mercer. We understand he's in every morning."

She shook her head. "You know, it's funny you should ask. He's usually over here as regular as clockwork, but I haven't seen him for a few days now. Maybe he's making breakfast at home." She tucked her order pad into her apron pocket and headed off to put in the order.

I wrapped my hands around my coffee mug to warm them after the chilly car ride over. "So much for Calvin's alibi for Tessa's death."

Grayson nodded. "I feel like I need a recap of everything we know at this point. Do you think you could help catch me up to speed?"

"Sure." I tried to organize it all in my brain. "So we've got Rachel Campbell who worked for Tessa Hayes at the county manager's office. She uncovered some financial irregularities in grant applications and municipal projects."

"Right. Then she mysteriously dies in what appeared to be an accidental drowning."

I said, "Exactly, even though Rachel was an excellent swimmer; she'd been on her high school swim team."

Grayson said, "We've got a few suspects for Rachel's death. Her husband, Andrew Campbell, who had financial problems that were solved by Rachel's life insurance policy. Andrew also lied about knowing Ethan Roberts. Andrew had actually gone to Ethan's office seeking investment advice."

I nodded. "Then we've got Wade Hartwell who was having an affair with Rachel. We need to find time to speak with him."

"And I guess his wife is also a suspect. At least, that's what Calvin thought. Julie could have been furious about the affair and might have blamed Rachel for it."

I said, "Plus, Rachel was a close friend of Julie's. She likely felt betrayed by her."

"Going back to Wade," said Grayson. "We now know he wasn't out of town at all when Rachel died. In fact, he was at Rachel's house earlier that day." He frowned. "Okay, that's most of what was going on with Rachel's personal connections. But we know there's a whole other group that had motives."

"Well, we do have one more on the personal end of things. Calvin Mercer, the rejected suitor. Rachel was clearly not interested in pursuing a relationship with him. Maybe Calvin lashed out at her," I said.

Grayson nodded. "Makes sense. Even if he says he accepted her romantic rejection, he still visited her grave years later. And now we know he lied about his alibi for Tessa's murder. He wasn't here having breakfast at all."

"And last but not least, we have Ethan Roberts. He gets defensive talking about his municipal dealings. Plus, his company keeps showing up in those questionable transactions. And I keep thinking about that tear in his coat sleeve when we were at the botanical gardens. It makes me wonder if it could have happened during a struggle with Tessa Hayes."

Grayson said, "Right. And it's all connected to what happened with both Dawson Blake's and Tessa Hayes' deaths. Dawson talked to Calvin about what he overheard in the county manager's office regarding these grants. The day before Dawson dies, he tells Calvin he has proof of something."

"It sure seems like it must all be connected to Rachel's discoveries at town hall, doesn't it?"

Our food arrived at the table, my grits creamy and perfect. Grayson's omelet looked stuffed with feta and spinach, his hash browns crispy on the outside.

"I'm surprised Rachel didn't tell anyone what she'd discovered about the financial irregularities earlier. If she had, maybe things wouldn't have turned out the same way," said Grayson.

"Maybe she needed to take some time to try to figure everything out," I said slowly. "She must have been checking and rechecking that information she'd uncovered. It had to have been stressful. It was her job, after all. And she could have lost her job if it looked like she was accusing her employers of something illegal, especially if it turned out she was mistaken about what she was looking at."

We finished up our food, quieter now, as we mulled over the different suspects. Grayson looked ruefully at his watch. "I hate to wrap this up, but I've got to go." He caught Heather's eye and paid up.

"I'll drop you by your house," he said as we walked to the car. We were halfway to my house when he said, "I know what I was meaning to tell you. Dawson's memorial service is tomorrow."

"Is it?" I asked in surprise. "I wasn't sure if Burton had reached out to Dawson's brother. I was starting to wonder if you and I should host a small memorial of some kind for him."

Grayson nodded. "I know. But apparently, he got hold of him. I've been meaning to tell you because I know you don't read the paper's obits. It's tomorrow afternoon. I can't remember—are you working then?"

"No, I'm working tomorrow morning. Today's my afternoon shift."

Grayson said, "I'll try to make the memorial service, but tomorrow might be kind of sketchy." He grimaced. "I want to be there to honor Dawson's life and represent the newspaper. But I've heard the furniture mill workers are planning a protest at the town hall tomorrow afternoon. One of my reporters is still out sick and another is covering a county commissioners' meeting."

"It sounds like you need to make the protest," I said. "I can pass on your condolences to Dawson's brother, if you like. Or get his address in case you want to write a note."

"Yeah, I may have to get you to do that, worst case scenario. But I'd still rather make at least part of the service. I'll let you know what time the protest ends up being tomorrow. The organizer is supposed to get back to me on that."

Grayson hurried off to get to work, and I set about to enjoy the rest of my morning with Fitz in a somewhat lazy fashion. I had a cup of coffee and curled up on my sofa with my cat and my book. No one called or texted, and it was heaven.

Back at the library that afternoon, I was relieved to see everything seemed pretty quiet. The printer was behaving itself and the patrons seemed deeply involved in books, studying, activities, or quiet conversations.

I caught sight of Owen sitting at a table with Timothy, hunched over what looked like math problems. Timothy was patient, explaining something step-by-step while Owen nodded. The defiant set of Owen's shoulders had softened somewhat, although he still looked wary.

Luna walked up to the desk. "Timothy is tutoring now?" she asked, gesturing toward the boys with her purple-streaked head. "Is there nothing he can't do?"

I explained Owen's background quickly. "It's something we're trying out. So far, so good. At least, from what I can tell."

Luna said wryly, "Hey, at least you came up with a better solution than Zelda. I bet she'd have called the cops on Owen the next time she saw him trying to break into cars."

"For sure. The only way he escaped that fate is because I promised her I'd call Burton myself. At first, we weren't sure we could get Owen over here because of the hours his mom works, but then Timothy's mom offered to help out with transportation."

Luna glanced back over at the children's section as it started quickly filling up with moms and toddlers. "I better run. Time for storytime. But I did want to let you know that Owen has been checking out our teen graphic novel section like he wants to read something. I have the feeling he doesn't have a library card yet, though."

I smiled. "I can fix that."

Before I could head over there, Zelda appeared, presumably to do her volunteer shelving. She paused, hands on her hips and her head cocked to one side as she watched Owen and Timothy. Zelda spotted me and gave a curt nod of approval. "At least somebody's keeping an eye on him now," she muttered before grabbing a cart of books to shelve.

I had the feeling Owen was going to have a lot more people monitor him than he'd bargained for. But that wasn't such a bad thing.

Chapter Eighteen

The next morning, I was back at the library, sans Fitz this time, since I was leaving straight from work to Dawson's memorial service. I had no idea if Grayson was going to be able to make it or not, even at the point when I was clocking out. I hadn't heard a word from him, which led me to believe that he'd gotten snowed at work.

The memorial service was held at the funeral home on Main Street, a modest brick building with white columns. I signed a guest book resting on a table near the door, alongside a framed photo of Dawson and fresh flowers. I'd just settled into a cushioned pew when Grayson came in, somewhat breathless and red in the face.

"You okay?" I murmured as he slid into a seat beside me.

He squeezed my hand briefly. "Yeah. Just broke away from a meeting and sped over here. I can only stay for the service, not the reception, but I'm going to try to speak with Dawson's brother before I leave."

The service started. Dawson's brother James, who'd flown in from Seattle, spoke haltingly about childhood memories. He was in his late-sixties with a thin frame and stooped shoulders.

His thinning gray hair was combed back neatly. James choked up a bit as he said he and his brother hadn't been as close, either geographically or emotionally, as they'd been when they were kids. But that he'd always been very proud of his big brother.

James's emotion made me tear up a bit myself, and I wasn't alone. The small group of attendees, mostly retired newspaper staff and a few people I recognized as library regulars—looked choked up, too.

The funeral director asked if any others would like to say a few words. I hesitated, feeling I didn't really know Dawson well enough to qualify. I was relieved when Grayson stood up and headed over to the lectern. He spoke about Dawson's dedication to uncovering the truth, his interest in investigative journalism, and his skill as a reporter. James looked pleased.

Afterward, before everyone headed to Quittin' Time for the reception, Grayson spoke briefly to James and shook his hand before hurrying out the door. I walked the short distance from the funeral home to the restaurant, shoving my hands in my pockets to keep them warm.

It felt almost surreal being at Quittin' Time again—my third visit there in twenty-four hours. The restaurant had put out a sandwich tray, a selection of personal-size bagged chips, and coffee and lemonade. They also had another table that was serving as a coffee station with regular and decaf, cream and sugar at the ready.

I spotted Harry Miller, Dawson's former coworker, there. His white hair was neatly combed and his round face was more subdued than usual. He gave me a gentle smile when he saw me.

"Ann," he said quietly, very different from his usual booming voice. "Dawson was one of the good ones, you know. Never met a story he couldn't get to the heart of." His blue eyes, though dimmed by the occasion, still held their characteristic warmth. "I'm glad you and Grayson are looking into things. Dawson would've appreciated that—having fellow truth-seekers carry on his work." He gave my hand a quick squeeze before another older man pulled him into conversation.

I grabbed a sandwich, chips, and a drink, then headed to a table near the window, figuring I'd eat while waiting to speak with Dawson's brother.

Andrew Campbell approached my table, coffee cup in hand. "Mind if I join you?"

I gestured to the empty seat, noticing he looked more relaxed than he had during our previous conversations. He settled in, then took a sip of his coffee.

"I didn't realize you were a friend of Dawson's," said Andrew, looking at me curiously.

"I didn't realize you were either," I said, wiping my mouth after taking a bite of my chicken salad sandwich.

"Touche," said Andrew wryly. "And, as I've mentioned before, I wasn't a friend of Dawson's, exactly. But it's hard living in the same small town for decades and not have at least a passing acquaintance with someone."

"That's the same with me. Dawson was a regular at the library."

Andrew nodded. "No surprise there."

I decided I might as well strike while I had the opportunity. "Speaking of being acquainted with people, I was surprised to learn that you had at least a passing acquaintance with Ethan Roberts."

Andrew frowned, his eyebrows knitting. "That's incorrect. As I mentioned, I don't know Ethan."

"Well, he knows you. At least, he's met you. He said you came to his office looking for help with investments."

Andrew blustered, "Oh, it was *that* guy? I'd totally forgotten his name. Anyway, that was ages ago. How am I supposed to remember that?"

"You do remember Tessa Hayes, though?"

Andrew looked down at his coffee. "Yeah, of course. I didn't really know her, but Rachel worked for her, so I felt like I did. I heard what happened to Tessa. That's nuts."

"What did Rachel make of Tessa?"

Andrew shrugged impatiently. "You're asking me to remember something from ten years ago again. How am I supposed to know?" He sighed, drumming his fingers on the table for a few moments. "From what I can remember, which isn't much, Rachel's feelings about Tessa and her work changed while she was there."

"In what way?"

He shrugged again. "She was crazy about Tessa at the beginning. I guess she looked at Tessa as a mentor. She talked about how cool it was to work for a woman who was high up in local government. I mean, I kept telling Rachel not to keep working as hard as she was. It wasn't like Rachel was getting a lot of money or bonuses or anything for all the hours she was putting in. It was pointless."

It sounded to me like Rachel had lots of respect for Tessa and wanted to do a good job for her. Maybe she thought it would lead to bigger things. Tessa was influential and if Rachel impressed her with her work, then Rachel might have figured it could mean a more important role for Rachel later on. "What changed?"

Andrew snorted. "Well, it definitely wasn't the hours Rachel was putting in. In fact, the unhappier she got at work, the longer she was going through files. It drove me crazy. She wasn't even cooking supper anymore."

I raised a single eyebrow at this, and Andrew had the grace to flush and look away. It seemed to me that Andrew, who by all accounts was hopping between jobs all the time, perhaps should have been the one to cook. At least some of the time, anyway. "Did Rachel tell you why she was suddenly unhappy at the office? Or why she was going through files for so long?"

"I didn't ask and she didn't offer to tell me," said Andrew in a clipped voice. "I figured it was some sort of new project that had been dumped on her, like usual."

I changed course. "Were you surprised to hear of Tessa's death?"

"Well, of course I was. It's not like you're expecting a middle-aged woman to suddenly die. It was shocking to me, even though I didn't know her, just like I said."

"What were you doing day-before yesterday? In the morning?"

Andrew gaped at me. "Are you thinking you're some kind of detective?"

"Not at all. I'm just trying to help Grayson with some investigative journalism."

Andrew took another long sip of his coffee. "I was out fishing then. That's the nice thing about being your own boss. I can take time off work when I need to."

Since Andrew seemed defensive, I decided to calm him down with some questions about his fishing. I figured it might also be a way to trip him up if he wasn't telling the truth. "Where do you like to fish?"

It seemed to work. Andrew leaned in closer. "I take my boat out on the lake. There are all kinds of trout there. Rainbow trout, brook trout, brown trout. And the water is crystal-clear."

"I wouldn't have thought the fish would be biting much in February."

Andrew scoffed. "You obviously don't fish much."

"No, I can't say that I do."

Andrew said, "I can catch fish anytime. Besides, the lake is quiet this time of the year, especially at this cove I go to. That's my favorite spot this time of year because the trout congregate there where the creek feeds in. I use a special setup—downrigger on the boat to get the lure down about thirty feet where the big ones are holding. I had my usual spread of a couple of flatfish lures. You've got to troll slow, maybe 1.5 knots, zigzagging across the drop-off."

I wasn't sure exactly what Andrew was talking about, but he did sound convincing. He clearly enjoyed fishing and must certainly have done it. The question was whether he did it when Tessa died. Once again, I felt like I should shake things up a little.

"I spoke with someone who mentioned Rachel had been having an affair," I said slowly.

Andrew sighed. "This town," he said. "It's just full of gossips. Yeah, it's true. But I didn't know anything about it. I only found out after Rachel died when Julie Hartwell told me about it. There I was, grieving Rachel, and Julie came up to tell me Rachel had been unfaithful to me."

"That must have been awful."

Andrew nodded. "It was. I felt totally betrayed. I thought our marriage was in great shape. If Rachel hadn't been happy, I wish she'd just told me. That way, we could have tried to work things out."

He turned to look behind him at the spread of sandwiches. "I wasn't hungry when I came in here, but I think I am now. I might just grab one and go."

I had one more question for him. "Before you head out, is there anyone you can think of who might have done this?"

Andrew gave a barking laugh. "Done this? You mean killed three people? I really couldn't say. I'd like to think I don't know any murderers at all. They're absolutely sure Dawson and Tessa were murdered?"

I nodded.

Andrew drummed his fingers on the table again, thinking. "Well then, I guess I'd have to say Julie Hartwell. She had every reason to be angry with Rachel."

"I understand the two of them were good friends."

Andrew said, "They were the *best* friends. Rachel was always hanging out over at Julie's place, and vice-versa. I always saw as much of Julie as I did my own wife. And if they weren't visiting in person, they were texting each other or on the phone together."

"So it must have been a real shock when Julie found out her husband was having an affair with Rachel."

Andrew spread out his hands. "It must have been. Like I said, I didn't know anything about the affair until Julie told me about it. But she was really hurt. I could see her killing Rachel, but I have no idea why she'd have gone after Dawson and Tessa."

"Maybe they'd uncovered the truth about Rachel's death."

Andrew said, "Yeah, I guess. Which makes sense in regard to Dawson. The guy was a reporter. But Tessa? I just can't see it. Anyway, I'm going to head out. See you later."

He stood and started heading away from the table as I scanned the restaurant to look for Dawson's brother so I could speak with him. Before Andrew could get far from the table, a stocky man with a friendly demeanor approached him. I recognized him as Hank Miller. He worked part time at Quittin' Time and part-time at a boat repair shop and also occasionally came to the film club at the library.

"Hey man," said Hank loudly to Andrew. The noise in the restaurant had built up, not just because the retired newspaper reporters had switched to beer, but because other diners had come in. "Glad to see you here. Just wanted to give you a heads-up that your boat will be ready for pickup in a couple of days."

I froze. It sure didn't sound like Andrew had been fishing on his boat yesterday. Not unless he'd just dropped it off at the shop yesterday afternoon.

I saw Andrew had frozen as well. Hank continued, blithely unaware, "Sorry it took us a while to get it done. We had some other jobs we were finishing up."

"No, it's fine," said Andrew. He started moving toward the door again, but Hank continued.

"I'm afraid it's going to be a big bill, but you know how boats are. We replaced pistons and rebuilt the carburetor. Should be working like a breeze now."

Andrew suddenly pivoted, looking in my direction. I glanced down at my plate, where the remains of my sandwich lay, holding my breath. I felt his gaze on me for a few moments before I saw movement out of the corner of my eye. I let my pent-up breath go as he left.

Chapter Nineteen

I stood up, feeling just shaky. That look Andrew had shot me felt malevolent. He must have seen me looking at him, listening in on his conversation with Hank. I suddenly wanted to leave the restaurant and head back home to Fitz. I spotted Dawson's brother James and quickly headed in his direction to speak with him before I left.

James gave me a smile. "Thanks so much for coming."

I explained my connection with Dawson, how he'd been a respected regular patron at the library. Then I hesitated before saying, "I'm friends with Grayson, too. Grayson talked about what a great journalist Dawson was. In fact, he and I are trying to unofficially look into Dawson's death, from perhaps a different angle than the state police are coming from."

James's eyes sparked with interest. "A different angle? What do you mean?"

"We think Dawson's death might be connected with something he was investigating. But because what he was looking into was a cold case, the police are looking at other options first before they start investigating a death from ten years ago."

James nodded slowly. "Rachel Campbell's death."

"You know about it?"

"Dawson, being a reporter, was quite a letter writer," said James with a bit of a hollow chuckle. "It's primarily how we kept up. He would always say he was tired of getting just junk mail and bills in his mailbox. So we'd write each other back and forth."

"And Dawson wrote you about Rachel?"

James nodded slowly, reaching into his suit for the interior pocket. "I'm going to give this to the police, but have a look before I do, since you're looking into things, as well. I got Dawson's last letter the day after he died." James's voice trembled just a little over the last words.

The envelope was worn at the edges, as if it had been opened and read multiple times. I took it from James carefully. The paper inside was covered with Dawson's distinctive, cramped handwriting.

"He always did favor that old reporter's shorthand," said James sadly. "Even in family letters."

I scanned the letter, trying to make sense of Dawson's cryptic notes: *"Think I know why someone's been invisible in plain sight all these years."*

I frowned at that. "And you don't have any idea who Dawson was referring to? Maybe someone he spoke about during previous letters?"

James shook his head. "I'm afraid not."

I returned to my reading. *"Found something in the old grant files. The same pattern keeps showing up. Someone's been playing the long game here, Jimmy. And I think Rachel stumbled on it, too."*

The use of "Jimmy" made me give a sad smile. Dawson obviously wanted to share his excitement with his brother without revealing too much.

"Did Dawson usually share details of stories or investigations he was working on?" I asked.

James rubbed his face wearily. The last week must have been such a strain on him; losing his brother in such a violent way, having to plan a memorial, flying across the country. He said, "Not really. He'd just share bits and pieces—you know, enough to tell me what was on his mind. But this was different. His tone was a lot more urgent."

"I know he was technically retired," I said.

James snorted. "Yeah, that didn't seem to work out so well, did it? I guess it was hard for Dawson to stay away from journalism. It's what he spent his whole life doing."

"What was he doing after he retired and before he started working on this story?"

"Oh, this and that. He'd try to pick up a new hobby, then he'd drop it. He started trying to cook for himself, but lost interest in that. Then he thought he'd travel but didn't have the income. He puttered around in his yard some, but wasn't really into gardening and yard work. The latest thing was woodworking," said James.

"Woodworking? Did he ever mention Calvin Mercer, by chance?"

James frowned. "I can't say I remember. But it wouldn't have seemed like something important to me, either—just another hobby of Dawson's. I could check some of my other letters when I get back to Seattle. He only started with the woodworking a couple of months ago, so he hadn't had time to give up on the hobby yet."

"Do you mind if I take a picture of this letter?" I asked.

"Not at all. I hope it can help you find out who did this. Dawson was a good guy and a great brother. He didn't deserve any bit of this."

Someone came up to talk to James, and I quickly handed him back the letter after taking a picture. He smiled sadly at me and turned away.

I drove away from Quittin' Time, heading for home with relief. Suddenly, I just wanted to climb into some comfy clothes and curl up with Fitz while drinking a cup of herbal tea. The service had been lovely, but tiring, and I felt bad for James, who'd clearly cared a lot for his brother. Then there had been the interaction with Andrew, and his lie about fishing when Tessa died. Of course, other suspects hadn't been totally upfront, either. But Andrew's reaction, that feeling of malevolence I'd gotten from him, had been unnerving. All in all, it had been an emotional afternoon.

I checked my phone for messages once I'd parked at home. There was nothing from Grayson, which wasn't surprising, since he'd said he was going to be slammed. So I headed inside, shedding my memorial service clothes for a soft pair of joggers and a tee shirt. Fitz had been napping in a sunbeam, and he stretched and yawned before changing his napping spot to the sofa, where I was taking up residence with my tea.

I wanted to spend a few minutes thinking things through. I pulled up the picture of Dawson's letter to James and read through it again. I could practically feel the energy through

Dawson's words. There was no doubt he was excited about his investigation and what he was finding out. It sounded like he was on the verge of a real breakthrough. It made me sad. Dawson was trying to help solve a murder and, in the process, was murdered himself.

Fitz looked solemnly at me from his position on my lap. I put the phone away and rubbed him for a few minutes. I sighed. "You're right, Fitz. Maybe I need to take a break from all this for the rest of the day. I thought it would be better if I mulled it all over, but it's just making my mind go in circles."

Fitz gave me an understanding look before curling up in a ball to go to sleep. I was tempted to follow suit, but read my book and drank my tea instead.

I was startled when my phone rang, and Fitz jumped, too. It was Grayson, immediately apologetic. "Sorry I had to bail before the reception today. Did it go okay?"

"It went fine."

Grayson said, "Good. I'd love to get filled in on it later. But I have a random question for you now. I know you mentioned we should talk with Wade Hartwell about his affair with Rachel. I just called him up a few minutes ago, telling him I was doing a piece on Rachel's death."

"How did he take that?" I asked wryly. "I'm guessing he doesn't want his affair with Rachel mentioned in the newspaper."

Grayson chuckled. "Yeah, probably not. But he did seem to want to set the record straight, whatever that might entail. He said he could meet us at his office—he's still working at that architectural firm downtown."

"When?"

"Right now," said Grayson, sounding apologetic again. "Want me to swing by and pick you up?"

"I'll be ready."

Fitz gave me a disappointed look as I extricated myself from the sofa and him. "Sorry, sweet boy. I'll be back before long." At least, I thought I would be. I couldn't imagine Wade Hartwell wanting to prolong the time he spent at work for too long.

The firm was housed in one of Whitby's historic buildings, all gleaming wood and brass fixtures. Wade's office was on the second floor, with large windows overlooking Main Street. He stood when we entered—a tall man in his mid-forties with graying hair and an expensive suit. His handshake was firm, professional, giving nothing away.

"Please, have a seat," he said, gesturing to the chairs across from his desk. Architectural drawings were spread across the surface, weighted down with brass paperweights. "Grayson mentioned you had some questions about Rachel Campbell for the paper."

I noticed he said her name without hesitation, as if he'd made peace with it long ago.

"We do," said Grayson. "Some new information has come to light about her death."

Wade's expression didn't change, but his fingers drummed once on his desk before going still. "That was a long time ago."

"Ten years," I agreed. "But we now know you weren't out of town that day like everyone thought."

Now there was a reaction, a slight tightening around his eyes. "Who told you that?"

"Does it matter?" asked Grayson quietly.

Wade was silent for a long moment, staring out his window at the street below. Finally, he said, "Julie knew, didn't she? She must have seen my car."

"Why did you lie about being away?" I asked.

He turned back to us, and I saw something vulnerable flash across his face before it was replaced by his professional mask. "Wouldn't you? I was having an affair with a married woman who turned up dead. Of course I gave myself an alibi."

"What really happened that day?" Grayson asked.

Wade rubbed his face wearily. "Rachel called me early that morning. She was upset and said she needed to talk. I'd been planning to go to Charlotte for a client meeting, but I post- poned it." He paused. "When I got to her house, she was already agitated. She was pacing, actually. She said she couldn't do it anymore. Any of it. The affair, her marriage, her job."

"What was wrong with her job?" I asked, leaning forward.

"She wouldn't tell me specifics. Just that she'd found some- thing, and she didn't know what to do about it." He gave a hol- low laugh. "I thought she was being dramatic. Rachel could be intense sometimes."

"What time did you leave her house?"

"Around eleven, I think. She said she needed time alone to think." He shook his head. "I should have stayed. Maybe if I had, none of this would have happened."

"Did she mention going out on the boat?" asked Grayson.

"No. Absolutely not. Rachel hated that boat and wanted to sell it. She said Andrew spent money they didn't have on it, then barely used it. She told me Andrew had found out that she was planning on selling it and was furious." Wade's face darkened. "I always thought that was strange, her being out there alone on that boat. I wondered if Andrew might have argued with her out there, blew up, and killed her because she was wanting to sell the boat."

I exchanged a glance with Grayson. "Did you know Dawson Blake?"

"The reporter? Not really. He interviewed me once years ago about a restoration project." Wade frowned. "I heard he was murdered. Terrible thing."

"And Tessa Hayes?"

Now Wade looked genuinely confused. "Tessa? Of course I know her. Everybody does. She has an important position in this town. And, naturally, we worked on several municipal projects together." He gestured to a framed rendering on his wall showing a downtown development. "What does she have to do with this?"

"She's dead too," said Grayson. "Murdered, like Dawson."

Wade went very still. "You think they're connected? To Rachel?"

"We do," I said. "Did Rachel ever mention anything specific about work? About grants or municipal projects?"

He was already shaking his head. "She was very professional about work stuff. She wouldn't discuss details." He paused. "But now that you mention it, there was something. That last morning, she kept saying 'The numbers don't add up.' Over and over. I thought she was talking about her life. You know, metaphorically. But maybe she was talking about work." He trailed off, looking troubled.

"Did you love her?" I asked quietly.

Wade's professional demeanor cracked slightly. "Yes," he said softly. "Not the way I should have loved my wife, but yes. Rachel cared about doing the right thing, even when it was hard." He looked down at his hands. "I've regretted a lot of things in my life, but loving Rachel wasn't one of them. Letting her down: that I regret."

"Where were you when she died?" Grayson asked.

"At the office. I came straight here after leaving her house. I worked late to catch up on things, then stayed here at the office" He looked at us wryly. "I was supposed to be out of town, right? I did try to call Rachel a few times, but she didn't answer." His voice grew rough. "I went back home the next day, mid-morning. I found out Rachel was dead when Andrew called Julie. I was in my study at home when I heard Julie shriek." He glanced at his watch. "I think I've told you all I can. You're welcome to use what I've said as background information, but I don't want any of it mentioned in the paper. Not attributed to me, at any rate." It was definitely a dismissal.

After we left Wade's office, I turned to Grayson. "What do you think?"

"I think he cared about Rachel," said Grayson. "But I don't think he killed her. And his reaction when we mentioned Tessa's death seemed genuine."

I nodded. "And he basically admitted to the affair right away. No more lying about being out of town." I paused. "What he said about Rachel hating the boat fits with what Calvin told us about her never using it."

"One more piece suggesting her death wasn't an accident," said Grayson grimly. "That somebody led her into a trap."

The weight of the day's revelations was catching up with me. Between the memorial service and that draining interview with Wade, I felt exhausted. Grayson must have noticed because he suggested driving me home.

I was going to invite him in, but he'd caught me unsuccessfully repressing a yawn a couple of times in the car. He gave me a kiss and a tight hug, telling me to get some rest. Considering I had an early start for work the next day, I was happy to comply.

Chapter Twenty

Back at the library the next day, my mind drifted back again to Tessa's death, especially the revelation that Andrew Campbell hadn't been fishing at all the morning she was murdered. If he'd lied about that, I wondered what else about that day wasn't adding up.

I was helping a patron find books on container gardening (he was dreaming of summer, although it was February) when Luna appeared at my elbow, her purple-streaked hair unusually disheveled. Today she was wearing what looked like three different floral patterns layered over each other, topped with a cropped denim jacket covered in patches.

"Ann," she said in a stage whisper that carried across half the library. "I need your help. It's an emergency."

The patron I was helping smiled indulgently. Most of our regulars were used to Luna's dramatic pronouncements by now.

"Just let me finish up here," I said, leading the patron to our gardening section. Once he was happily browsing, I turned to Luna. "What's the emergency?"

"Jeremy and I made our vacation lists like you suggested." She pulled two crumpled pieces of paper from her jacket pocket. "But they don't match up. At all."

"Let me see," I said, smoothing out the papers on the reference desk. Luna's list was written in at least five different colors of ink, with little doodles in the margins. Jeremy's was typed, with bullet points and sub-categories.

"See?" Luna threw up her hands. "He wants to go hiking in national parks and looking at rocks. *Rocks*, Ann! While I want to go somewhere with art galleries and music festivals and street food."

"Well," I said diplomatically, "at least you both want to travel domestically. That's something."

Luna slumped against the desk. "Jeremy says we need to be practical about the budget. But I say if we're finally taking a vacation, we should go somewhere amazing." She lowered her voice. "I think he's worried about investing too much money on something I plan. You know, after that time I tried to organize the library carnival and accidentally booked both a mariachi band *and* a bagpipe player for the same time slot."

I tried not to smile at the memory. The resulting musical clash had been rather memorable. "Have you two sat down together and actually talked about what you each want from this vacation?"

"We tried last night. But then we got distracted by this documentary about penguins, and then Jeremy started talking about maybe we should go see penguins, but I get seasick so Antarctica is definitely out, and then—" She took a breath. "Anyway, we got nowhere."

Just then, Jeremy himself walked in, carrying what looked like a stack of travel guides. He brightened when he saw Luna, then looked slightly sheepish when he saw us staring at all the books.

"I thought maybe we could do some research," he said, setting the books down. "You know, find somewhere that has both outdoor activities *and* cultural attractions."

Luna's face softened. "You went to the bookstore?"

"Actually, I got these from Timothy," Jeremy admitted. "He's been everywhere with his family and had some suggestions."

I started looking through the stack. "Look at this one—Asheville. It has mountains for hiking, but also lots of art galleries and music venues. Plus it's right down the road."

Luna peered over my shoulder. "Ooh, they have a food tour. And look at all the street art."

Jeremy pointed to another page. "There are some really interesting geological formations in the area. And lots of waterfalls."

"Waterfalls are definitely more romantic than rocks," Luna conceded. She looked up at Jeremy with a grin. "Remember our first date when we went walking in the rain?"

"And you insisted on splashing in every puddle?" Jeremy smiled back at her. "How could I forget?"

"Maybe that's your theme," I suggested. "Water. Mountains. Art. Food. Find a place that combines all of those things. And going someplace close is like a mini-vacation—a trial run for the real thing."

Luna's eyes lit up. "We could make like a vacation mood board. Jeremy, we could make lists of activities we each want to do, then trade off days. One day hiking and waterfall-hunting, the next day galleries and food tours."

"As long as you don't try to book us with three different tour groups at once," Jeremy teased.

"That was *one time* with the mariachi band," Luna protested, but she was laughing.

"Why don't you two grab a study room?" I suggested. "Isn't it your break, Luna? You can spread out all these books and start planning properly."

They gathered up the travel guides, but Luna paused before following Jeremy. "Thanks, Ann. You always know how to make things make sense." She lowered her voice again. "And thanks for not mentioning that time I accidentally booked the traveling circus performers for the children's reading hour. The library board still brings that up at meetings."

I watched them head off to the study room, already deep in discussion about possible itineraries. Through the glass, I could see Luna gesturing animatedly while Jeremy nodded, taking notes. They were an unlikely pair, but somehow, they made it work.

Kind of like me and Grayson, I thought with a smile. Though at least Grayson and I had planned a few trips to Charleston with no mariachi-bagpipe incidents.

Fortunately, the library was not its usual bustling self. Aside from Linus in the periodicals section, making his way through the newspaper and a patron who'd nodded off in the reference area, the library was dead.

I pulled up the archives of *The Whitby Times* to see the news around the time of Rachel's death ten years ago. First, I found the newspaper edition for a couple of days after Rachel died. They'd run a story about her drowning death on the front page. Obviously, the news of her death had come too late for the story to make the paper the morning following her death.

Then I pulled up the edition from the day Rachel drowned. I felt my pulse quicken when I saw Stan Matthews, a reporter and photographer for the paper, had taken several photos of the marina to cover the start of the boating season.

I clicked through the images, seeing boats gleaming in the spring sunshine, a couple of kids fishing off the pier, and people readying their boats for the summer. Then I stopped, my hand frozen on the mouse. In the background of a shot showing a family securing their boat cover, a familiar van was visible at the far end of the marina parking lot. It was Calvin's distinctive workshop van with its hand-painted logo—the same one still parked outside his shop today.

According to the article, Stan had spent "a perfect after-noon" on April sixteenth at the marina photographing the seasonal activity. Calvin had told us he was at a woodworking symposium demonstrating lathe techniques that entire day. But there was his van, at the marina, the same day Rachel died.

I sat back from the computer. Surely Calvin remembered where he was that day. He'd said he loved Rachel. He wouldn't have forgotten his location on April sixteenth. The whole day had probably been emblazoned on his memory. Was he just trying to cover up the fact that he'd been nearby since Grayson and I were looking into Rachel's death?

Now I had both Andrew Campbell and Calvin Mercer who'd lied about their whereabouts, although for different murders. Calvin had also said he'd been at Quittin' Time when Tessa died.

Thinking back to the other suspects, Julie Hartwell had admitted driving by Rachel's house the day of the murder. And she'd spotted her husband's car there, so Wade Hartwell certainly wasn't where he was supposed to be. Ethan Roberts had been very vague about his whereabouts for both Rachel's and Dawson's death.

I saved screenshots of what I'd found. I was about to dig deeper into the archives when Timothy appeared at the reference desk. "Ann, can I talk to you a minute? It's about Owen."

My heart sank. "Is everything okay?"

"Well, that's the thing. He didn't show up for our study session this morning. His mom called looking for him. She actually dropped him off this morning, not my mom, but apparently Owen never came inside."

My mind leaped over to the memory of Owen trying car doors to break into vehicles. "Are you sure he's not in the library? You checked the stacks?"

"And the reading nooks and the study rooms. Everywhere. Then I remembered he'd been really interested in the graphic novel section, so I checked there, too."

Before I could panic further, Zelda appeared, still wearing the shirt from the auto repair place with her name on it. She must have overheard us because she narrowed her eyes. "The boy's missing? I'll start patrolling the neighborhood."

"Wait," said Timothy suddenly. "I just had a thought. Yesterday, Owen was asking me about the old Carnegie library plans we have displayed in the historical room. He was pretty interested in the building's architecture."

The historical room was tucked away in an attic room on the second floor. It was rarely used except by researchers and people who were looking for complete and utter silence. "Let's check it," I said.

We found Owen sitting cross-legged on the floor, surrounded by old blueprints and architectural drawings. He flushed, looking guilty.

"I know I missed our session," he said in a rush to Timothy. "But look at this. The original plans show all these secret spaces in the walls. They had to make room for the heating systems back then."

Timothy sat down on the floor next to him, examining the drawings. "These are really detailed. Are you interested in architecture?"

Owen shrugged, trying to look offhand, but his expression was eager. "Maybe. I like how everything has to fit together just right. Sort of like a puzzle." He traced one of the lines on the plans with his finger. "And I like that you can see how everything's supposed to work."

"Unlike people?" asked Timothy in a quiet voice.

Owen's shoulders hunched slightly. "Everything made sense before my mom moved us here. Now it's like nothing does."

Zelda glanced over at me. I was just relieved she hadn't immediately started fussing at Owen for disappearing. It seemed like the boy was working through a lot of stuff.

"I get how everything is confusing," said Timothy. "I felt the same way when I started homeschooling. I had a tough time with the other kids at school, too, so my mom pulled me out."

"You were bullied, too?" Owen looked up at Timothy in surprise.

"Yeah. I'm not saying the change to the collective was easy. It was weird at first, not having a normal schedule like everyone else." He shrugged. "It's not for everybody. But it worked out for me. I realized I could learn at my own pace and focus on stuff that really interested me."

"Like computers?" asked Owen. "I'm interested in those, too."

Timothy nodded. "Exactly. And now I get to help other people with their tech, too." He grinned. "Speaking of which, I noticed yesterday you were helping Mrs. Logan with her tablet settings when she couldn't get her e-reader to work."

Owen shrugged again. "She was getting frustrated. I just showed her how to adjust the font size."

I finally spoke up. "You did a great job helping her, though. You gave patient, clear instructions. Just like Timothy does during the tech help sessions."

"Would you maybe like to help out during the next session?" asked Timothy. "We could always use another tech-savvy person on the team."

Owen's whole face lit up before he caught himself and tried looking casual. "Yeah, I guess. If you need the help."

"We do," said Timothy firmly. "And maybe afterward, if you're interested, I could show you some basic coding. You know, if you want to learn how apps and websites actually work."

"Really?" Owen couldn't contain his excitement this time. Then he looked worried. "But what about our regular tutoring?"

"We'll still do that, too," Timothy assured him. "But I think you're ready to add some extra projects. Maybe we could even create a 3D model of the library on the computer, showing all those hidden spaces you found." He paused. "But for now, we probably need to head back downstairs and get our regular schoolwork done."

"Yeah," said Owen, giving me an apologetic look. "Sorry that I disappeared. Does my mom know?" He looked worried.

"I'll call her," I said quickly. "And you can hang out up in the historical room anytime. Just let somebody know where you are, okay?"

Owen nodded, then he and Timothy headed downstairs, Owen still asking questions about 3D software. I heard Timothy explaining different programs as Zelda and I followed them from a distance.

"Well," said Zelda with satisfaction, "at least the boy's not breaking into cars anymore. Though somebody needs to talk to him about proper sign-in procedures for the historical room."

I hid a smile. "I'm sure you'll be happy to explain the rules to him."

"You bet I will," said Zelda. But her tone was more proud than stern. "Imagine—we might have a future architect or engineer on our hands." She frowned. "Although he better not get any ideas about redesigning the neighborhood. "Those original Victorian facades are historically protected."

Back at the reference desk, I abandoned looking at the archives and delved back into library work. Suddenly, a slew of patrons came inside, all needing help with devices, research on medical conditions, or how divorce proceedings work.

When I next looked up at the clock, it was past time for me to have lunch. Wilson was gesturing to me from his office, indicating I needed to abandon my post and take it. He did like things to run like clockwork.

That, unfortunately, was the moment I realized that in my hurry to get me and Fitz out the door this morning, I neglected to grab my bag lunch. Which meant I'd have to spend most of my lunch break hunting down food and spending money I really didn't need to spend.

I was just grabbing my coat to head out on this scavenger hunt for a place that wasn't too expensive and didn't have a long line when Grayson hurried into the building, his cheeks pink from the February cold. Not only was I delighted to see him, I was delighted to see the two takeout bags he was holding. Fitz trotted up to weave himself in between Grayson's legs. He reached down to scratch him under the chin.

He gave me a relieved look. "I didn't think I was going to catch you before you started eating."

"I forgot my lunch today," I said ruefully. "You've totally saved the day."

"Well, hopefully not the *day*, but at least your lunch hour. Should we go to the breakroom?"

I nodded, leading the way so I could swipe my badge to get in there. Fitz happily padded behind us. It was a small area with a smattering of books, various houseplants, a kitchenette, and

plenty of sunbeams coming from the tall windows. Fitz immediately took up residence in one of the sunbeams. Grayson and
I plopped down in some old wooden chairs covered with vinyl
cushions that had come from the main section of the library before a long-ago renovation.

Grayson handed out deli sandwiches, small containers of
potato salad, and cookies, along with napkins and plastic cut-
lery. He frowned. "I forgot to order drinks."

"No worries. We have water here. Or would you rather have
coffee?"

Grayson stood up, "I'll get coffee. A blast of caffeine is sorely
needed. Water or coffee for you?"

"Water, please."

We settled down and were companionably quiet for a few
moments while we ate. Grayson and I were apparently pretty
hungry because I eliminated my chicken salad croissant and he
his pimento cheese on rye in no time.

I took a big gulp of water to wash everything down before
starting on my potato salad. "I'm glad you're here. How are
things going at work?"

Grayson grimaced. "It's still chaos, but I see a light at the end
of the tunnel. I'm hoping things are going to calm down late this
afternoon. We're fully-staffed again, so that's something. I was
about to draft one of the retirees from the memorial service if
things hadn't gotten any better soon."

I smiled. "I bet they'd have loved that, actually. Getting
called up from retirement."

"True. Maybe another time. This is sure to happen again."

I said, "I found out some stuff. Andrew Campbell sat down with me at the memorial service reception yesterday. He gave this thesis on fishing, which he'd claimed to be doing during the time of Tessa's murder. Then I overheard a conversation between him and Hank—the guy who works at the boat repair place, as well as at Quittin' Time. Apparently, Andrew's boat is in the shop and has been for some time."

Grayson's eyes widened. "Seriously? Wow. That's the second lie he's told us, then. He'd also said he didn't know Ethan, even though he'd had a meeting with him."

"Right."

Grayson looked uneasy. "Did Andrew realize you'd overheard something that negated his alibi?"

"It's possible. He swung around, but I looked down and acted like I hadn't heard anything. I'm not sure if he bought that or not. Then, this morning, I went through some of the newspaper archives and found articles from around the time of Rachel's death."

Grayson gave me a wry look. "You'd have thought I'd have taken care of that."

"Well, you've had a lot going on at work. I don't know how you've been able to juggle things as well as you have. Anyway, I found photos taken the afternoon Rachel drowned. Calvin Mercer's van was at the marina. So it appears he couldn't have been at that symposium he was talking about."

Grayson leaned forward. "Another lie from Calvin. He also said he was at Quittin' Time when he wasn't."

"Exactly. So I guess we need to double back around and talk to these guys again. And, if I get a quieter afternoon at work, I can call Burton and get him caught up, too. I'm thinking by now that the state police are probably looking at other options for Dawson's death, especially considering what happened to Tessa."

Grayson glanced at his watch. "How about if we talk to Calvin after five? I should be leaving the office around then. We could just casually follow-up on what you've found out. More fact-checking than accusations."

"Sounds good. I'll meet you over there," I said. "I don't have to close up tonight because I opened the library this morning."

"Perfect."

Chapter Twenty-One

The rest of my lunch break was spent deliberately talking about lighter topics. Grayson talked about the inconvenience of his broken coffeemaker. Keep Grounded had been chockful of people when he'd desperately forged his way in before going to the office. Then, he'd somehow managed to walk away with someone else's order.

Grayson gave me a light kiss before we left the breakroom. Fitz opened a drowsy eye when he saw us open the door. "Want to come out? Or hang out in the sunbeam for a while?" I took him closing the one eye back as a sign he preferred his peace and quiet, at least momentarily. Then Grayson headed out, and I became immediately engulfed in helping a frazzled patron format her resume. "My interview's in forty-five minutes," she said, twisting her hands. "And none of the bullet points line up."

I quickly knocked the resume in shape, giving the poor woman time to get back home and change before her interview started.

The afternoon turned into one of those times when I just couldn't seem to catch my breath. An elderly gentleman kept tapping random buttons on his tablet, undoing everything I showed him about downloading ebooks. Luna's voice carried from the children's section, "Ann! We've got a storytime situation." That turned out to be fifteen more toddlers than expected, all of whom were armed with tambourines and annoyed looking moms.

I'd just gotten the noise level down to a dull roar when a patron started fussing at me because of an overdue fine. "I know exactly when I returned that book. I refuse to pay a fine." And, as I was forgiving the fine on the computer, the Wi-Fi chose that moment to give up the ghost, causing a chorus of groans from every corner of the library.

I glanced at my watch when I could catch my breath and saw it was already a couple of minutes after five. I found Luna. "Hey, Fitz is still wandering around the library, if he's not still in the breakroom. I'm meeting up with Grayson for a quick errand, but I'll be back as soon as I'm done to collect him, okay?"

"Of course. You know I love that little guy. Hey, I was going to update you on Jeremy's and my vacation plans, too."

I could tell Luna wanted to talk. And I did, truly, want to hear her out. But I was already running behind to meet up with Grayson and visit Calvin Mercer again. "I promise I want to hear all about it. But I'm running really late right now."

Luna quirked her eyebrows. "Is this about the case?"

I nodded, and Luna said, "Well, why didn't you say so? Hurry up and go! I want justice for Dawson."

Fitz came ambling up as I grabbed my bag, and Luna scooped him into her arms, tickling him under his chin as his eyes closed happily. "See you soon, Luna," I said in a rush as I hurried for the door.

But the universe was apparently determined to keep me from meeting up with Grayson. I was fumbling for my keys in the dim light in the parking lot when I heard a gritty voice behind me. "Ann. I've been waiting for you."

I whirled around to see Andrew Campbell. "Why?" I asked, sounding pretty gritty in return. I backed away from him, right into the side of my car. Then I looked around, trying to see if anyone was nearby. But although the parking lot was full, no one was currently coming or going. Fumbling for my keys again, I kept my finger over the alarm button on my key fob. I knew from past experience when accidentally hitting it, its screech could wake the dead.

"I think you might have overheard something you didn't understand at Dawson's memorial service," Andrew said.

"What's that?" Playing dumb, I figured, might be a way to make Andrew spell it all out.

He looked annoyed. "You heard the boat repair guy saying my boat is in the shop."

"Is it? That must be inconvenient. Especially when you said you were on it when Tessa was murdered."

Andrew's face grew red with anger. "I knew you were going to misunderstand that."

"Oh, I think I understand perfectly. You said you were somewhere you weren't. Then your alibi was disproven."

Andrew said harshly, "I was asleep that morning, okay? I wasn't even awake, much less out killing people I don't know. I just thought saying I was out fishing would be more believable. So what you overheard means *nothing*, got it?" He moved menacingly closer to me.

Which was when he was hit over the head by a golf umbrella wielded by Zelda. She whacked him with what must have been all of her strength and continued doing so until Andrew, wincing and holding his arms up to protect his head, backed away.

"What're you doing?" Andrew howled at Zelda.

Zelda didn't deign to answer him. "I'm calling the cops, that's what I'm doing. I recognize assault when I see it."

"Yeah, assault is what you just did to me!" yelled Andrew.

Zelda swung the enormous umbrella at him again, and he quickly ducked before jogging off to his car.

"Thanks," I said to Zelda. "You don't have to call the cops, though. I'll do that, myself. I meant to catch Burton up on everything, but just didn't get around to it during work."

"Nope! I'm still going to call Burton and tell him what I saw. He needs to know this town is going to hell in a handbasket." Zelda was puffing with indignation or perhaps some shortness of breath associated with her chain smoking.

"Whatever you need to do. And thanks again, Zelda. I owe you one."

Zelda's eyes lit up at this. I realized after I said it that being in Zelda's debt was probably not the best place to be in. Also that I'd forgotten to get my house key back from her. But I really needed to go, since I was now very late to my meeting with Grayson at Calvin's. I hopped into my Subaru and drove off, being careful not to speed, since Zelda was on a tear when it came to illegal behaviors.

I quickly called Burton, but got his voicemail. I left a voice mail message explaining my encounter with Andrew and his failed alibi. Then I told him about Calvin's lies about being a the woodwork symposium the day of Rachel's death and being at Quittin' Time when he'd clearly not been there for a while. I signed off, saying that I was meeting Grayson at Calvin's workshop to ask some follow-up questions.

Burton called me back as I was driving. I gave him a rundown on what had happened with Andrew Campbell in the parking lot and how his alibi had fallen through. I also gave more information on Calvin's van being at the marina the day Rachel died. Burton made some irritated growling sounds on the other end of the line.

"Hold up a minute, Ann," he said, sounding tired. "I need to get this straight."

"What do you need?"

"The state police want a timeline. They're still somehow focused on Dawson's recent activities, his family connections, anybody who might have had a grudge. But you're pretty positive we need to look back ten years."

"Three deaths, Burton. All connected to Rachel's case."

He sighed. "I know. But the state boys don't want to devote resources to a cold case when we've got active homicides to solve."

I heard papers shuffling on his end. "The state police are treating these as separate cases. Dawson could have been killed by someone connected to any story he wrote over his career. Tessa had enemies from her position. But my gut says you're right about the connection."

"Your gut and the evidence," I pointed out.

"Yeah, well, my budget won't stretch to a full cold case investigation right now. And the state police . . . " He trailed off.

"Let's just say they're not interested in theories about decade-old drownings. They want concrete evidence connecting these deaths."

"So what do we do?"

Burton was quiet for a moment. "You and Grayson keep digging. But Ann? Be careful. Whoever this is, they're cleaning house. First Dawson gets too close to the truth, then Tessa. I don't want you or Grayson being next."

I thought about the malevolent look Andrew had given me in the parking lot. "We'll be careful," I promised.

I heard someone calling Burton's name in the background. "Look, I've got to go," he said. "The state police want another briefing. But Ann? Document everything. If we're going to convince them to look at the cold case angle, we need solid evidence."

I hung up the phone. Burton's hands were tied by bureaucracy and budgets, while the state police were wearing blinders. Meanwhile, someone in Whitby was killing to keep their secrets from becoming public.

When I got to Calvin's workshop, it seemed very quiet there. It was already dark, since the sun sets so early in February. As expected, Grayson's car was already there. Something made me close my car door as quietly as possible. I chided myself for being paranoid, but then it made sense I would be, considering what had just happened in the library parking lot.

I slipped up to the side of the workshop, deciding to play it safe and peek into the window before knocking on the door.

When I did, I saw Calvin holding Grayson at gunpoint both of them standing very still and looking very pale.

Chapter Twenty-Two

My heart was pounding so hard that I felt like Calvin and Grayson might hear it. I fought through it so I could think. I quickly texted Burton, afraid to talk aloud. Then I silenced my phone. Was there time to wait for Burton, though? And why would Calvin point a gun at Grayson if he didn't mean to use it? If he was the killer, he'd already murdered three times before. I'd be a fool to think he wouldn't do it a fourth.

Grayson was backed against Calvin's workbench, facing me. Calvin, pointing the gun, had his back to me. Going through the door looked like it was out; Calvin would be able to see me come in. I desperately tried the window, hoping it wouldn't squeak as it opened. To my relief, it slid open quietly. Calvin must keep everything oiled.

Grayson's gaze slid briefly sideways to see me, then immediately looked away to keep Calvin from turning to look behind him. Luckily, Calvin seemed deeply involved in trying to exonerate himself of the murders and explaining how everything had been a terrible misunderstanding. I felt a chill go over me hearing his voice, which was just as modulated and precise as when talking about woodworking.

"You're looking at this all wrong," he said to Grayson. "Rachel's death was an accident. An awful accident. I tried to save her, but it was too late."

Grayson's voice was steady. "You went a little further than just Rachel."

Calvin shook his head. "I didn't have a choice with Dawson or Tessa."

I was halfway over the windowsill, waiting for Calvin to continue talking and cover up any noise I made dropping to the floor. But he seemed to be deep in thought. Grayson was studiously avoiding looking at me, his face white.

"What happened to Rachel?" asked Grayson.

Calvin's voice was heavy. "She drowned, just like they said. I didn't lay a finger on her. I was here in my workshop and spotted her on the boat, a little ways out from my cove. I have my own boat, and I took it out to anchor next to her. We never had much time to talk at town hall because she was always working, and I was trying to get grant money."

"Everyone said she hated that boat," said Grayson, clearing his throat. "Did you find out what she was doing there?"

"Rachel was selling the boat. She said she'd taken a few pictures of it in the marina, then decided to take it on the water when the sun was setting to help it sell. She told me she and Andrew could use the money and the boat loan was in her name." Calvin now sounded scornful. "Andrew's credit was too bad for him to get a boat loan, so Rachel applied for it herself."

Grayson said in an almost casual voice, "What happened when you had that conversation with Rachel? You asked her out?"

Calvin gave a short laugh. "Well, she was married, so not really. It's not like we could go out to dinner together, could we? Not in a small town like this. Somebody would have told Rachel's husband right away. But I did try to convince her that she needed to leave Andrew. I told her I could provide her with a better life—the kind of life she deserved."

I was looking around the workshop, my gaze darting from one thing to another, looking for anything I could use for a makeshift weapon. The neat rows of tools on the pegboards were too far away. So was the wood, stacked precisely by size and type. Then I spotted a can of wood varnish on a shelf nearby. The lid was already loosened, as if Calvin had been working with it earlier today. In fact, now that I was focused on it, the chemical smell was sharp in the cool air of the workroom.

Grayson was still being very careful not to look in my direction and give me away. He kept Calvin talking while I reached slowly for the varnish can. "Was this the first time you told Rachel your feelings?"

Calvin, still facing away from me, nodded. "Yeah. It wasn't the sort of thing I needed to say at town hall, right?"

"And how did she take the news?"

Calvin said sadly, "She looked like she felt bad for me. That's all I really saw. Pity."

I grasped the can, carefully removing the lid. Then I said sharply, "Calvin."

He spun around, and I threw the contents of the can right at him. The varnish caught him full in the face. He stumbled backward, dropping the gun as he clawed at his eyes, coughing and gasping.

Grayson grabbed the gun, training it on Calvin. "Don't do anything stupid," advised Grayson in a shaky voice.

I could hear sirens in the distance.

"Hope those are for us," said Grayson grimly.

"They should be. I texted Burton a few minutes ago." I paused, watching Calvin trying to wipe his eyes, which must have been burning quite a bit. "I hope they bring an ambulance along. He's going to need to flush his eyes out." I picked up my phone again and made a call, just in case.

Calvin was sitting hunched over on the floor. I said, "What happened next? With Rachel?"

Calvin said quietly, "A boat went speeding by—a much bigger vessel. It made the water choppy in its wake, plus the wind had kicked up, which wasn't helping. Rachel lost her footing, slipped on a wet spot on the deck, and came off the boat into the water, falling in-between our boats. She hit her shoulder on the side of the boat on the way. I heard her gasp when she hit the water. She might have taken in water." He rubbed his sleeve across his eyes. "She never came up."

"Did you jump in? Try to find her?" I asked.

"Of course I did," said Calvin scornfully. "I jumped right in. I kept diving down under the water, over and over again. The wake was making the boats bob and drift around like crazy. I opened my eyes underwater, but the visibility in the lake was awful, and the sun was rapidly setting. There was no sign of her."

I said, "I know you said she'd been an excellent swimmer."

Calvin's voice was hoarse with emotion. "That's why it was so hard to accept that Rachel was gone. When I finally accepted that I couldn't find her, I got back in my boat and docked it.

didn't want anybody to get the wrong impression and think that I'd hurt Rachel. I'd *never* have done that."

I heard cars slide to a stop outside. A moment later, Burton was inside the workshop, taking in the scene of Grayson pointing a gun at Calvin. He cuffed Calvin, reading him his rights. Somehow, though, Calvin now seemed almost relieved that it was over. It was quite a change from his violent attempt to protect himself from exposure earlier. But maybe, deep inside, his crimes were just as abhorrent to him as they were to others.

"What happened here?" asked Burton quietly.

We caught him up quickly. Calvin listened, looking intent. And a little ashamed.

Burton nodded as we wrapped up our narrative about what got us to that point. He regarded Calvin thoughtfully. "Got it. What I'd like to know, is how Dawson ended up figuring out you might have something to do with Rachel's death. From what I've heard, it sure sounds like he was on the trail of financial irregularities at the county."

"Oh, he was," said Calvin calmly. "Dawson was going to uncover all that fraud. I guess he went down a rabbit hole with that stuff—but then he came to realize that Rachel's death wasn't because someone in town hall or an unscrupulous developer was trying to shut her up."

Burton cocked an eyebrow and said, "It was because of you."

Calvin flushed, looking miserable. "It wasn't *directly* because of me. I was trying to offer a life to Rachel. I wanted us to make a life together. Andrew wasn't any good for her. She was *supporting* him, for crying out loud. The guy couldn't hold down a job to save his life. I'd have taken care of Rachel. Cherished her.

He'd never have done that." His mouth twisted. "I hate him for profiting off her death."

It made me wonder if Andrew Campbell might have been Calvin's next victim if he hadn't been stopped. I could see the fury in his face as he thought about him.

Burton must have noticed it too, because he was looking thoughtfully at Calvin again. "Back to Dawson and how you both ended up at the abandoned warehouse."

Calvin looked down again. "Dawson was onto something. Yeah, he was investigating the financial stuff, but that had led him in my direction."

"How was that?" asked Burton.

Calvin sighed. "I do restoration work on wooden boats, so I have a monthly maintenance agreement with the marina. Dawson was digging around at the marina."

Grayson frowned. "The marina? What would that have to do with the county manager's office?"

Burton answered that one. "The marina is town property. Maybe he was looking to see if there were irregularities there, too."

Calvin nodded. "Yeah. In the process, he looked on the marina log and saw I'd signed into the marina for routine maintenance the afternoon Rachel died."

I said, "Although you'd told everyone you were demonstrating lathe techniques at a woodworking symposium."

Calvin shrugged. "When you started asking questions, I figured that was the best way to clear myself of suspicion. That way, I put myself far away from the lake."

Burton said, "Okay. So Dawson came over and started asking you questions. He probably did the same thing Ann and Grayson did: spoke to Tessa and found out you'd been looking lovelorn over Rachel. Maybe Dawson asked you where you were when Rachel died, and you came up with your alibi."

"The symposium," I said dryly.

"Right. So Dawson would want to find out why you were at the marina when you'd said you'd been at a symposium. I'm guessing you decided that was too much of a risk. You followed him, thinking you'd better get rid of him."

"Maybe I just wanted to talk to Dawson. Convince him to leave it alone," said Calvin.

"Like you just wanted to talk with Rachel?" asked Burton. "That didn't turn out so that great last time."

Calvin ignored this. "The funny thing is that Dawson was tailing Tessa Hayes. He was so caught up in following her that he didn't notice I was doing the same thing to him. Very discreetly, of course."

"What on earth was Tessa doing at the warehouse?" asked Burton.

Calvin said, "I'd been waiting in town hall for grant information and overheard some talk about the warehouse being torn down and the land possibly repurposed. I'm guessing she was out there to do a quick assessment to see what that might entail. Dawson, I think, was looking for a quiet opportunity to catch her on her own and find out what she knew about the financial irregularities he'd been looking into."

"Dawson followed Tessa. You followed Dawson," said Burton. "So how did Tessa get roped into all this?"

"She must have forgotten something at the warehouse when she left. Of course, I kept my van out of sight while she and Dawson were inside. When Tessa left, I went inside the warehouse to talk to Dawson."

Burton quirked his eyebrow again. "Talk."

"Which is what it started out as. You know what ended up happening. Dawson wouldn't accept that I'd made a mistake about where I was the day Rachel died. I mean, it was a decade ago—my memory wasn't perfect. When he wouldn't let it go, I had to force him to be quiet." Calvin looked solemn but defensive.

"Okay. Then Tessa came back? She saw you there?" asked Burton.

"No. But when I was driving down that old road to leave, she saw my van. Maybe she'd left something at the warehouse—her phone or something. Anyway, she saw the van heading away from the warehouse area. It wouldn't have meant anything to her that day. Maybe she even thought I had another job out that way. I drive all over town."

I said, "But it would have seemed a lot more significant when she realized somebody killed Dawson."

Burton nodded. "So Calvin, you had to clean up again. Tessa was a loose end."

Calvin looked defensive again. "What was I supposed to do? Just let her go to the cops? Turn me in? If I got rid of Dawson, I needed to get rid of Tessa, too."

"I'm not sure a jury is going to see it the same way," said Burton with a grim smile. His deputy motioned Calvin to the door and escorted him out.

Burton turned toward us. "Now, how are the two of you?"

My heart still felt like it was beating too fast. And I felt really alert, like I was paying attention to the slightest thing.

"I'm just really glad to be alive," said Grayson slowly. "And that Ann turned up at exactly the right time." He shook his head. "You're never late anywhere. If you'd been on time, you and I would both be dead right now." The color was still drained from his face, and the stress showed in worry lines on his forehead.

Burton said, "Andrew Campbell actually did you a favor, didn't he?"

"What?" asked Grayson, looking confused.

I gave a short laugh. "Andrew Campbell tried to threaten me in the library parking lot when I was trying to leave. He wasn't happy that I knew he had a fake alibi for Tessa's death." I shrugged. "It doesn't matter now. But he wanted to let me know that I better keep quiet about it."

"He didn't hurt you, did he?" asked Grayson, his features darkening.

"No. No, *he* was actually the one who got hurt. Zelda didn't like the way he was talking to me and beat him up with the biggest umbrella I've ever seen."

"An umbrella? There hasn't been any rain for a week or more," said Grayson, eyes crinkling.

"You know how Zelda likes to be prepared."

Burton said, "I have the feeling Andrew Campbell isn't going to file assault charges against Zelda. Seems like that's something he might want to keep under his hat." He glanced at his watch. "I'd better head to the station. I want to be there when the state police come in. We'll be wanting to match up those hairs we found at the scene of Dawson's murder."

"What about all the financial irregularities Rachel and Dawson uncovered?" I asked Burton. "The grant money, the shell companies, the double-billing?"

Burton nodded. "The state police financial crimes unit is taking that over. They've already started auditing all the municipal projects from the past decade. From what they're finding, it looks like a few developers and contractors were gaming the system, but it wasn't as widespread as Rachel initially feared. They'll be looking into our friend, Ethan, too." He gave a tired smile. "Good thing the state police will be on it. I don't have the manpower to investigate both murders and municipal fraud."

He reached out and squeezed us both on the shoulder. "You two go get some rest. You deserve it."

As soon as Burton said that, I did suddenly feel very tired. Exhausted even. Like I wanted nothing more than to hibernate the rest of this cold, dark February.

Then Grayson reached out a hand to me, and I took it. "Meet you back at your place?" he asked gently. I nodded.

I barely remembered driving back to the house, apparently on autopilot as I went. It was a moonless night, and the temperatures had dropped when the sun set. I somehow beat Grayson back to my house, and fumbled with icy hands to get my house keys out.

Then I closed my eyes, wincing. Fitz was at the library, of course. I'd asked Luna to keep an eye on him, thinking I'd make a brief trip to Calvin's. Which obviously got completely derailed.

Grayson was pulling into the driveway as I stepped toward him, keys in hand. He rolled down his window and looked at me with a quizzical expression. "Make yourself at home," I said. "I've somehow totally lost my mind and left Fitz at the library."

"I'll get him," said Grayson quickly.

"No, I'll do it," I said, but he was already backing up his car and driving away.

I went inside, figuring I'd use the time to start a fire in the fireplace. When I opened the door, though, I discovered a small collection of notes that had been methodically slipped under my door throughout the day. They were written in Zelda's distinctive handwriting, a precise, angular script that somehow managed to convey both authority and indignation even in simple messages. Each had the time noted in the top right corner, underlined twice for emphasis.

The first had apparently been delivered early in the morning: "10:15 AM - While conducting morning patrol with your key, observed suspicious door-to-door salesman. Lingered precisely 2.3 minutes longer at #42 than at other homes. Highly suspicious. Have documented description (blue golf shirt, khaki pants, receding hairline). Will maintain vigilance."

The next message had come in the afternoon: "2:30 PM - Used key to verify home security during midday neighborhood watch. All secure. However, Mrs. Henderson's Christmas lights are STILL up. This is a February violation of Section 3, Paragraph 2 of the HOA guidelines. Have photographic evidence."

A third note was written on the back of what appeared to be a gas station receipt: "3:45 PM - Spotted three unswept walkways while doing follow-up patrol. Your sidewalk, however, meets HOA standards."

The final message had been delivered just before I got home: "4:45 PM - Completing last patrol of the day. Returning key with submission of full surveillance report. Have drafted complete documentation of all observed violations. BTW - your gutters could use attention (Section 5, Paragraph 8)."

My house key was taped to this last note with a piece of neon orange duct tape that screamed "violation." Beneath it was a meticulously detailed spreadsheet documenting every neighborhood infraction Zelda had spotted during her "patrols." It included timestamps, photographs, and specific HOA bylaw references. At the bottom was a PostScript: "Have you reconsidered joining the HOA board? Think about it."

I couldn't help but smile as I removed my key from its orange tape prison. Trust Zelda to turn borrowing a simple house key into a full-scale neighborhood reconnaissance operation. At least I had it back now, though I had a feeling I'd be getting follow-up reports about that suspicious salesman for weeks to come.

I suddenly wanted all the cozy things, what the Dutch call hygge. So I put on my great aunt's kettle to boil for tea, got the fire going with some seasoned kindling, and then dug in the freezer until I found the soup I'd frozen. I started defrosting it in the microwave so I could heat it on the stovetop more easily.

I'd thought Grayson might be back by then, but he likely got caught up talking with Luna, who always had the propensity to be quite chatty. I changed out of my work clothes and into something much softer. I must have been hoping that the combined cozy setting around me would cocoon me somehow.

I was just putting the soup on the stovetop when I heard Grayson's car. A moment later, Fitz bounded through the door ahead of him, making his special chirping sound that meant he was happy to see me. Grayson set his empty carrier down inside the door, smiling at me.

"Sorry that took so long," said Grayson, shrugging off his coat. "Luna wasn't there, but Wilson was doing some late work. He helped me track down Fitz." He paused, taking in the scene: the crackling fire, the kettle whistling, the smell of soup warming. "You've been busy."

"Just trying to make things cozy." I lifted Fitz into my arms, burying my face in his fur for a moment. "It's been quite a day."

"It has." Grayson's voice was quiet. He came over and wrapped his arms around both me and Fitz, and we stood there for a moment, just breathing. The fire popped, sending up sparks, and Fitz purred contentedly between us. Then Grayson said, "You know what I was thinking about, watching you throw that varnish at Calvin?"

"That I have terrible aim?"

He chuckled, the sound rumbling against my back. "No. I was thinking about how much I love you. How I want to come home to you every night, not just the nights when one of us almost gets killed." His arms tightened around me. "I was thinking about how you're the first person I want to talk to every morning and the last person I want to see every night. How you make even the craziest days better."

I turned in his arms to face him, still holding Fitz. I was suddenly feeling so breathless that I wasn't sure I could get the words out. "Are you saying what I think you're saying?"

"I am." He reached into his coat pocket. "I've been carrying this around for weeks, waiting for the perfect moment. And I kept getting thwarted," he added ruefully. "First there was the music concert that Luna and Jeremy horned in on. Then a sudden rainstorm messed up the hike we were going to take. After that, the furniture mill closure when I had to cancel our dinner at Capri. Even this morning, I thought maybe after the gym . . . " He shook his head with a soft laugh. "But then I realized—this is perfect. Just us, and Fitz, and soup on the stove, and a fire in the fireplace." He pulled out a small box. "You're my favorite person to solve murders with, to drink coffee with, to talk about books with. What do you say? Want to combine our book collections permanently?"

I let out a watery laugh. "That's a pretty serious commitment. Have you seen how many books I have?"

"I have. And I love every overcrowded shelf." His blue eyes were warm in the firelight as he opened the box. "I love how you care about people, how you notice details others miss, how you make the library feel like home for everyone who walks in. I even love how you drink that terrible kale smoothie every morning at the gym." He took a breath. "Marry me?"

Fitz gave an approving trill as I said yes, and Grayson slipped the ring on my finger. Then he pulled me close again, Fitz purring happily between us while the soup simmered on the stove and the fire crackled in the hearth.

About the Author

B estselling cozy mystery author Elizabeth Spann Craig is a library-loving, avid mystery reader. A pet-owning Southerner, her four series are full of cats, corgis, and cheese grits. The mother of two, she lives with her husband, a fun-loving corgi, and a couple of cute cats.

Sign up for Elizabeth's free newsletter to stay updated on releases:

https://bit.ly/2xZUXqO

This and That

I love hearing from my readers. You can find me on Facebook as Elizabeth Spann Craig Author, on Twitter as elizabethscraig, on my website at elizabethspanncraig.com, and by email at elizabethspanncraig@gmail.com.

Thanks so much for reading my book…I appreciate it. If you enjoyed the story, would you please leave a short review on the site where you purchased it? Just a few words would be great. Not only do I feel encouraged reading them, but they also help other readers discover my books. Thank you!

Did you know my books are available in print and ebook formats? Most of the Myrtle Clover series is available in audio and some of the Southern Quilting mysteries are. Find the audiobooks here: https://elizabethspanncraig.com/audio/

Please follow me on BookBub for my reading recommendations and release notifications.

I'd also like to thank some folks who helped me put this book together. Thanks to my cover designer, Karri Klawiter, for her awesome covers. Thanks to my editor, Judy Beatty for her help. Thanks to beta readers Amanda Arrieta, Rebecca Wahr

Cassie Kelley, and Dan Harris for all of their helpful suggestions and careful reading. Thanks to my ARC readers for helping to spread the word. Thanks, as always, to my family and readers.

Other Works by Elizabeth

Myrtle Clover Series in Order (be sure to look for the Myrtle series in audio, ebook, and print):
Pretty is as Pretty Dies
Progressive Dinner Deadly
A Dyeing Shame
A Body in the Backyard
Death at a Drop-In
A Body at Book Club
Death Pays a Visit
A Body at Bunco
Murder on Opening Night
Cruising for Murder
Cooking is Murder
A Body in the Trunk
Cleaning is Murder
Edit to Death
Hushed Up
A Body in the Attic
Murder on the Ballot
Death of a Suitor

A Dash of Murder
Death at a Diner
A Myrtle Clover Christmas
Murder at a Yard Sale
Doom and Bloom
A Toast to Murder
Mystery Loves Company
A Murder Down Memory Lane (2025)
The Village Library Mysteries in Order:
Checked Out
Overdue
Borrowed Time
Hush-Hush
Where There's a Will
Frictional Characters
Spine Tingling
A Novel Idea
End of Story
Booked Up
Out of Circulation
Shelf Life (2025)
The Sunset Ridge Mysteries in Order
The Type-A Guide to Solving Murder
The Type-A Guide to Dinner Parties
The Type-A Guide to Natural Disasters (2025)
Southern Quilting Mysteries in Order:
Quilt or Innocence
Knot What it Seams
Quilt Trip

Shear Trouble
Tying the Knot
Patch of Trouble
Fall to Pieces
Rest in Pieces
On Pins and Needles
Fit to be Tied
Embroidering the Truth
Knot a Clue
Quilt-Ridden
Needled to Death
A Notion to Murder
Crosspatch
Behind the Seams
Quilt Complex
A Southern Quilting Cozy Christmas

MEMPHIS BARBEQUE MYSTERIES in Order (Written as Riley Adams):
Delicious and Suspicious
Finger Lickin' Dead
Hickory Smoked Homicide
Rubbed Out

And a standalone "cozy zombie" novel: Race to Refuge, written as Liz Craig